The Last Horseman

Frank Zafiro

Other Crime Series By Frank Zafiro

River City Series
Police procedurals with ensemble cast, begins with *Under a Raging Moon*

Stefan Kopriva Mysteries
Private detective mysteries, begins with *Waist Deep* (set in River City)

SpoCompton Series
Hardboiled underside of Spokane, begins with *At Their Own Game*

Cam & Bricks Jobs (with Eric Beetner)
Two competing hitmen – action and dark humor, begins with *The Backlist*

Ania Series (with Jim Wilsky)
Hardboiled noir with a femme fatale, begins with *Blood on Blood.*

Charlie-316 series (with Colin Conway)
Police procedurals full of action and intrigue, begins with *Charlie-316*

Jack McCrae Mystery Series
Retired detective solves mysteries, begins with *At This Point in My Life*

A Grifter's Song
Serial anthology series featuring a grifter duo (creator/editor/contributor)

Frank also writes mainstream fiction and non-fiction as Frank Scalise and science-fiction and fantasy as Frank Saverio!

The Last Horseman

A Sandy Banks Thriller

Frank Zafiro

Published by Code 4 Press, an imprint of Frank Zafiro, LLC
FrankZafiro.com

Cover design by Zach McCain

ISBN: 978-1-962889-11-7

For Steve Wohl, who planted the seed.

The sword of justice has no scabbard.

—Antoine de Rivarol,
French writer, 1753 –1801

Prologue

Gail Ridley poured the fresh-brewed coffee slowly into one cup, then the other. She savored the vision of the dark, steaming liquid as it filled each cup. The scent wafted up and she breathed it in.

She left room in each cup. She'd replaced the coffee pot, opened the cupboard and removed a bottle of Bailey's Irish Crème. With a small smile, she poured a generous amount into each, watching the dark brown liqueur spread throughout the black coffee, changing its color.

"Mom?"

"In here," Gail answered, twisting the top on the Bailey's and putting it away without hurrying.

Terri came into the kitchen, her expression drawn. "He's rambling again," she said, her voice tinged with sadness and weariness.

"What's he talking about?" Gail asked. She pointed at the service tray on the other side of the kitchen.

Terri followed her motion and retrieved the tray. "Police stuff, mostly. Names I don't recognize." She handed Gail the tray. "Some of it's hard to understand. His voice is so raspy."

Gail took the tray and said nothing. She loaded the cups onto it, then added a few macaroons and a paper napkin.

"He used to have such a deep, powerful voice," Terri said. She shook her head. "It makes me sad to hear it now."

"It's God's will," Gail answered her.

"Why would God want Dad to have throat cancer?" Terri asked. There was no malice in her voice. For a moment, it almost seemed to Gail that her daughter was eight years old again, standing in the kitchen, helping her make dinner and asking all sorts of difficult questions.

"I have no idea," Gail answered.

Terri smiled at her. "You're such a rock, Mom. How you deal with this, I don't know. If anything ever happened to Matt, I'd—"

"You'd handle it," Gail said. She returned her daughter's smile. "There's really no other choice."

Terri's smile broadened. She leaned over and kissed Gail on the cheek. "I've gotta go. The kids are out of school in half an hour and I have to brush up my résumé for an interview tomorrow."

"Good luck," Gail said. "And tell the grandbabies we love them."

"I will." Terri sniffed at the coffee. Her smile turned sly. "Mom…I don't think Doctor Hallett would approve of Dad drinking booze in his coffee."

Gail shrugged. "I really don't think it matters, dear," she said. "And besides, he doesn't usually drink it, anyway."

"Usually?"

Gail raised her eyebrows slightly.

"Okay," Terri said. "Mom knows best." She kissed Gail again and left through the back door.

Gail lifted the tray and made her way into the bedroom. Cal Ridley sat up in the bed, staring down at a photograph of himself. Ever since the cancer had spread to his brain, she'd witnessed wild fluctuations in his memory and cogency. The moments when he was just her Cal had dwindled and were rare now.

"Who's that handsome man you're looking at?" she asked,

setting the tray on the table beside the bed.

Cal cast her a look that was a mixture of irritation and fear. "It's me," he snapped. Then he added, "Isn't it?"

She smiled warmly. "Of course it is, dear. That is you. Lieutenant Cal Ridley on the day he graduated the police academy. Almost forty years ago."

"Lieutenant," he mouthed. He stared down at the picture for another long moment, then tossed it aside. "Lies," he said. "Too many lies."

Gail didn't answer. She knew he'd worked for years in the Narcotics Unit and the Vice Unit. Later, he'd supervised those same units. Drugs and Vice had to be the most distasteful parts of police work, she figured.

She lifted a cup of coffee and held it out to him. "Cal?"

He looked over at her, saw the coffee and shook his head gruffly.

Gail settled into the chair beside the bed. She sipped the coffee herself. The warmth of the liquor spread throughout her stomach.

"So smart," Cal said, his voice raspy and broken. "Thought we could bring justice to this world. Our world."

"You did," she said quietly. "You led a noble life, Cal."

His eyes snapped to her. There was a wildness in them that frightened her. Not for her own safety, but because of the distance in them. They were eyes that barely recognized her, or maybe not at all. And that foreshadowed what she knew was soon to come.

"The system is broken, Sandy," Cal said to her.

Who is Sandy?

"You're the right man for the job, though," he said. "You and Brian make four." Then he laughed and looked away. "The Four Horsemen of the Apocalypse. Except all of you are Death."

Gail didn't reply. The doctor told her that his words would

meander and seem nonsensical at times, almost as if his mind was dreaming while awake. He warned her that Cal might slip into speaking gibberish before the end. She could try to engage him, but he told her not to expect too much.

"Are you thinking about God, Cal?" she asked him.

He looked at her again. Recognition and warmth came into his eyes. "Ah, Gail. Did you just say God?"

"I did."

He smiled gently. "You know that I only went to church all those years because that's where you were, don't you?"

"Of course I know," she said.

He reached out to her. She took his hand.

"I just thought maybe you might be coming to God," she added.

His smile turned slightly cynical. "Me and God have an understanding," he said. "And it doesn't involve any last minute reprieves."

"You're a good man, Cal," Gail said. "And God forgives us all."

Cal squeezed her hand gently before releasing it. "Not those who play at being God," he rasped.

Gail didn't know how to reply. She sipped her coffee.

Cal stared out the window. "All the mistakes of a broken system. I tried to fix them. With my tools. My Horsemen. Hank. Bill. Sandy. And Brian." Tears formed in his eyes. "Brian was such a young pup. I shouldn't have brought him in. And then Sandy—"

He broke off, his Adam 's apple bobbing as he wept silently.

Gail put down her coffee. She took his hands, covering them with her own.

"I gave them all those cases," Cal rasped. "All those sonsabitches that slipped through." Tears streamed down his cheeks. "And they did what had to be done," he said. "They brought justice to bear."

"It's okay, Cal," she whispered. "It's all right, dear."

Cal didn't seem to hear her, yet he lowered his voice to a croaking whisper. "But there's no justice in the world," he said.

No, Gail thought. *There isn't.*

1

Ten years later

"It isn't right," Detective Randall Cooper muttered to absolutely no one. "It's not fuckin' right."

He stood in the back of the near empty courtroom as the judge droned on about the reasons for his whacked out decision. The words he spoke didn't matter to Cooper. What did matter was the result.

Jeff Odoms was going free.

Cooper shook his head, as if doing so would change the reality in front of him.

Jeff Odoms, the man who kidnapped two fifteen year old Japanese foreign exchange students from Riverfront Park, was going free.

The man who tortured them in his basement for three days with a riding crop and bared electrical wires from a lamp cord was going free.

The man who forced those poor girls to do things with each other that they had probably not even imagined doing with boys their own age was going free.

Cooper only half-listened as the judge spoke about the many flaws in the search warrant (the warrant he had written, goddamnit, and he *knew* how to write a search warrant). Phrases such as "lack of particularity" clanged in Cooper's ears.

Sure, he had rushed the warrant a little. Who wouldn't? Two girls were missing. They'd been missing for three days. Was he supposed to sit at his desk and tippy-tap type until every 'i' was dotted and every 't' was crossed? He didn't become a cop to be a clerk. He became a cop to catch bad guys and save lives. Not like that panty-waist judge up there.

And yeah, maybe his informant didn't have the cleanest record around. There were a few convictions for what the judge was calling "crimes of integrity." Joey Bitts was a thief. What'd you expect his record to look like? He sure as hell came through with good info on this one, didn't he? Just because he lied in the past, we have to throw out his statement?

"This is bullshit," Cooper muttered, wanting to scream at the judge.

He had good evidence on this case. He had the girls' statements, certified by a court interpreter. He had a witness who described the van the kidnapper used to snatch the girls and Odoms owned the exact same van. Once he got into the house, he found the electrical cord. He found the riding crop. Hell, he even found the videotape that Odoms made over the three days. The sick sonofabitch is on the tape sixteen different times!

You had it, he thought. Right up until one crack of the gavel from Judge Kravinski up there. Now it's all gone.

"In summary," Judge Kravinski said, his tone neutral, "the probable cause to obtain the warrant was insufficient due to the informant's failure to qualify as to veracity under the Aguilar/Spinelli doctrine."

Aguilar/Spinelli up your idiot ass, Cooper thought.

"Even absent that," the judge continued, "the warrant itself did not accurately describe the residence to be searched nor the items to be seized."

Cooper seethed. How am I supposed to know what I'm going to find until I get in there?

"The initial questioning of the defendant by Detective Cooper was done in violation of Miranda," Judge Kravinski said, glancing toward Cooper at that point, "and frankly, I have concerns that more than just the defendant's Fifth Amendment rights were violated during that interrogation."

Cooper returned the judge's stare, his jaw taut. Did he expect that someone like Odoms was just going to say, "Oh yes, detective, I did kidnap and torture those girls you found in the basement" or something like that? No, Cooper knew. Sometimes scum like Odoms had to be persuaded. Just a little.

"Without a doubt," the judge continued, "his Sixth Amendment rights were violated or at least delayed, since the detective's own testimony reveals that the defendant was not provided with an attorney immediately upon request."

Cooper shook his head again. He was supposed to serve up a defense attorney to this maggot as soon as he asked for one? Like a fuckin' cheeseburger?

"These are not, as the State has tried to argue, 'harmless errors.'" He glanced over at the prosecutor, who stood stone-faced, staring straight ahead. "Taking all of this into consideration," the judge continued, "I have no choice other than to suppress all physical and testimonial evidence obtained in this case, with the exception of the independent observation by the patrol officers in this case that a van matching the general description of the kidnapper's van was parked in the defendant's driveway."

For a brief moment, Cooper allowed himself to hope this might turn the tide. If the judge thought the van was enough for PC, then they could claim inevitable discovery and –

Judge Kravinksi adjusted his glasses and cleared his throat. "However, since this fact alone does not establish probable cause, I must reject the State's argument of inevitable discovery."

Cooper scowled. Figures.

The judge reached for his gavel. "All charges against the defendant are dismissed. He is released from custody." He dipped his gavel downward, rapping it delicately.

Cooper didn't wait to see Odoms turn to his scumbag defense attorney and smile. He couldn't stand the prospect of seeing the sick bastard's expression of self-satisfaction. Nor did he want to endure the accusing glare of the prosecutor on this one, either. That officious prick had already notified his sergeant about this case, calling Cooper "a buffoon with a badge."

No, he wasn't going to hang around for any of those pleasantries. Instead, he turned and barreled out the door of the courtroom and headed down the hall. He strode to the stairs and headed down them, stepping as lightly as his girth allowed. It seemed like he'd put on five or six pounds every year since he hit his twenty year mark. That put him at two-forty-five and twenty-nine years on the job. You don't spend that much time on the job without learning a few important lessons.

Like, there's more than one way to skin a cat.

Cooper reached the ground floor, his breath coming in little gasps. A sheen of sweat covered his head and neck, cooled by the air conditioning and his lumbering motion. Underneath his shirt, the sweat felt stickier and he caught a whiff of the sour scent of his armpits. He'd have to go up to the locker room and clean up before he headed back to the squad room. If his sergeant was going to rip him a new one, he might as well be daisy fresh for that dance.

But first he had a phone call to make. And it wasn't one he could make from the department phone at his desk.

There was something else Cooper had learned over the

years. Something only a few cops knew.
Something special.
Something about justice.

2

Sandy Banks strolled down the sidewalk with an easy stride. Although he kept his head erect and took note of everything in his peripheral vision, he did so more out of habit than any concern. It wasn't that danger didn't exist. He was just used to it. He'd walked too many battlefields and too many rough streets to be afraid of what *might* happen. He'd also learned there was enough that *did* happen to fill anyone's fear basket.

He glanced at his watch. Two-thirty-six. That was good. He tried to vary what time of day he came here every week when it was his turn. That was another habit and Sandy figured it was a good one.

He approached the post office at a steady gait. The crowd was heavy with late lunch traffic, but he'd always found this branch to be a busy one. Perhaps that was why Cal chose it, all those years ago. Hide in plain sight, in the midst of a crowd. Always a smart tactic.

When he entered through the front doors, Sandy's gaze swept through the interior. His mind clicked through what he saw, looking for anomalies. Any that he saw were negligible, just the rough edges of life. Nothing suspicious. Just men and women going about their business.

Sandy walked straight to the private mailboxes. He pulled his key from his jacket pocket and inserted it into the lock. Without pausing, he turned the key and opened the box.

There was a file curled up inside.

A momentary whisper of apprehension fluttered in his stomach. An image of cops in bad suits leaping out from behind the counter and around corners, pointing guns and yelling at him flashed through his mind.

He shook it off. If that was ever going to happen, it would have been in the early years. Now, the operation ran like clockwork.

Sandy reached up and pulled the manila envelope from the box, then snapped the metal door shut. Without hesitation, he turned and walked from the post office. Half a block away was a pay phone. He dropped a quarter in and dialed a number from memory. It rang three times, then picked up.

"Hello, this is Brian," the recording went. "Leave a message."

Sandy waited for the tone, then said, "This is the National Firefighter's Fund, collecting for fallen firefighters. We were hoping you'd like to donate. We'll try back another time. Thanks."

He hung up. He knew the message itself didn't matter. The sound of his voice was enough. Brian would know it was his turn to monitor the mailbox.

Back in his car, Sandy sat in the driver's seat. The weight of the envelope had a comfortable feel to it. He knew what to expect when he tore the edge open and slid the contents out. The first thing that would tumble out would be a thick stack of cash. Ten grand. Not enough to get rich, but enough to keep on.

More importantly, there'd be a file, thick with information about a very bad man. There'd be enough there to show Sandy what the bad man did and how he got away with it. And there'd be enough to find this bad man, whoever he was.

Sandy held off on opening the package. Instead, he slid his key into the ignition and started the car. There would be time enough for reading and planning and for killing soon enough.

3

"What are we going to do?"

Her voice irritated him a little, but only because she interrupted the relaxing quiet of the motel room.

"We've already talked about this," he said simply.

She shifted her leg, draping it over his. "I know, I know. But I want to be sure."

"You worry too much."

"You don't worry enough."

He smiled in the pale afternoon light that seeped through the curtains. "Opposites attract, I guess."

"I guess," she agreed.

She fell silent. He knew that she was waiting for him to fill the silence, just as he knew that she'd stay silent until he did. Any attempt to change the subject would be greeted with that silence, or at best, one or two word replies.

Her patience was greater than his, so he gave in.

"We go for it," he said. "What else are we going to do?"

She took a deep breath and let it out. "All right. I agree."

"Good."

"You're set to deliver the file?"

"Yeah," he said. "I'll do it tomorrow. Then we just sit back and let things unfold."

"How long, do you think?"

"How long does it usually take?"

She shrugged. "A couple of weeks, maybe. Sometimes less."

"Exactly."

"Why are you asking me if you already know?"

He squeezed her buttock with his hand, then gave it a light slap. "Why are you asking me when we both already know?"

"Nervous, I guess. This one's different."

"Not to the Horsemen."

"No," she said. "I suppose not." Then she asked, "What about the Odoms case?"

"I dropped it off yesterday."

"Good. That one is a sick son of a bitch."

He smiled slightly. "A sick son of a bitch who'd be in jail if Cooper wasn't a half-assed detective."

She sighed. "True. Maybe the Horsemen should deal with Cooper next."

He chuckled. "Let's keep them focused on the bad guys for the most part."

"Yeah," she said, settling her head onto his chest. "For the most part."

4

Sandy Banks sipped his diet Coke in the front seat of his blue Mazda. He stared up the street at an orange Chevy pickup truck with oversized tires. It was parked in front of the same bar it'd been parked in front of yesterday and the day before. Inside, Sandy figured that Troy Collins was no doubt drinking cheap domestic beer and shots. If he had to guess, he'd say that Collins was probably throwing a few lame pickup lines at the barflies collected there. Given what Sandy had learned about him over the past two weeks, the older ladies were probably getting most of the attention.

Over the past hour, stiffness had worked itself into Sandy's back. He shifted in the seat, but it didn't do much good. The motion only jostled his bladder and reminded him why he shouldn't drink caffeine when conducting surveillance.

He ignored the sensation and settled into his seat.

Was tonight the night?

He wasn't sure.

But he thought so.

There wasn't any specific reason for his optimism. Just the intuition that came from his days on the job and even more, since leaving. He'd developed a sense for these things early on. Timing was everything, and for what he was doing now, time was on his side. He could afford to wait for the perfect situation.

Actually, he couldn't afford *not* to.

Still, tonight felt good. Tonight felt lucky.

Sandy rested his head back against the seat, keeping his eyes locked on the front door of the grimy downtown bar. He didn't keep any files in the car with him, but he'd spent enough time at the storage unit memorizing what he needed to know about Troy Collins. And when he learned something new, he returned to the secret "office" housed in a storage unit and recorded it faithfully. Such things were habit for a retired policeman, true, but there was more to it than that. Keeping notes on targets was how he made sure to do things right. Getting the job done in the right way mattered. Besides that, it created a history. True, it was a history no one was ever going to read but he and the other Horsemen, but at least that way they knew what they were doing was right.

Troy Collins was his first case in several months. He was a worthy target. The file on him detailed his criminal history, which dated back to things Collins did when he was fourteen. Sandy knew that getting the juvenile records was no small feat, but then again, everything about what they did was no small feat.

Collins had been one lucky bastard, at least as far as Sandy could tell. His story was sprinkled with a seemingly unending supply of lenient judges, incompetent prosecutors, sharp defense attorneys, overzealous cops messing up procedure and victims unwilling to testify against him. The last category included a fifty-seven-year-old widow Margaret Thompson, who picked up Collins at a trendy north side bar that catered to more mature singles. Instead of the romantic interlude she expected at her home, she received a couple of hard slaps from Collins, who proceeded to rob her of $17,000 in cash and jewelry. After she reported him to police, Collins came back to her house, raped her and threatened to kill her if she didn't drop the charges against him.

Of course, Sandy knew no one would ever be able to prove the last part. The robbery detective that worked the case went up to see Margaret after she stopped returning his calls. She started by saying that she'd been mistaken about the money and jewelry. Then she broke down crying and told the detective enough for him to surmise what had happened. He tried to get Margaret to stay with family out of town somewhere until the trial, or barring that, to accept protective custody. But the terrified woman refused. She was certain that Collins would make good on his threat to come back and kill her.

Sandy took another sip of his diet Coke. He thought about it for the hundredth time. Then, for the hundredth time, he decided that Margaret Thompson was probably right about that.

The detective on the case was one Sandy didn't know. He might have been a patrolman before Sandy left the job, but he wasn't working in investigations. Nonetheless, he was a hard charger and not willing to let things go. He tried to go forward with the case based on Margaret's original testimony. True, it was essentially her word against Collins' word, especially since those slaps didn't leave any marks. But the detective testified to her statements regarding the threats and the rape, even though she denied them in a pre-trial hearing.

Sandy eyed the macho wheels on the truck Collins drove. He wondered if he used the money he robbed from Margaret to buy them.

The law is a funny thing, Sandy knew. It was a fickle and capricious beast. Every cop learned within six months that it wasn't what you *knew*, it was what you could *prove*. And that wasn't the last of it, either. It wasn't just what you could prove, but whether you played the game perfectly in the process of proving it. One mistake could derail an entire case.

The detective in the Margaret Thompson case tried to get her statement to him based on an exception called "excited utterance." The concept held that if people are under the influence of a significant emotional event, the things they blurt out tend to be true.

The prosecution argued that this was the state of mind Margaret was in when the detective interviewed her. Therefore, it should be an exception to the hearsay rule, even though she was denying those statements now. The detective should be able to testify about those statements.

The defense argued that it was not an exception. The defense argued that even if it was an exception, the court had its best evidence before it in the form of Margaret Thompson's direct testimony. And, of course, the defense argued that the detective was lying about Margaret's statement in order to bolster an already weak case against his most assuredly innocent client.

The judge sided with the defense.

Sandy swallowed the last of the diet Coke. He crushed the can and slid it into the plastic garbage bag on the floor of his passenger side.

With no victim willing to testify that there was a robbery, theft, threat or rape, the prosecution had virtually no case. Collins had been smart enough to hold onto the jewelry and not to pawn any of it, so there was no corroborative evidence. That left the prosecutor no choice but to drop the case.

Collins went free, having served only eleven days in jail awaiting the pre-trial hearing in which the prosecutor's motion to admit detective's testimony regarding Margaret's statements was denied.

Sandy knew that, if he were smart, Collins would have held onto the Thompson jewelry for a while yet. The detective might hang onto this case out of frustration. He might keep checking pawn records, or try to work on the victim to reconsider. Eventually, though, other cases would take priority. This one would get filed away as one of life's many unfortunate injustices.

And Collins would get away with it.

Hell, he might even go back and see Margaret again.

Except that Sandy knew he wouldn't.

Sandy remembered sifting through the Collins file at the office. All of the sins were catalogued on his rap sheet, lit up by the kerosene lamp for Sandy to see as he sat at the old battered desk with an open drawer. They'd filled one drawer with files and were deep into the second now. While Sandy never felt any joy at the time over how they solved those problems, a sense of righteous satisfaction always set in about six months or a year later. That was when he'd think about how justice had been visited upon the child molesters, the rapists, the murderers. It didn't matter to him how they were gone, just that they were.

When he read through the catalog of Troy Collins' misdeeds, he could feel the seeds of that satisfaction being planted. He knew what would make those seeds sprout and grow.

The Keeper didn't leave anything to chance. He held the Collins file for almost a year before sending it. He made sure to track several pawned jewelry items that belonged to Margaret Thompson back to Collins. Given his history of robbery and sexual offenses, the detective's investigation on the case and the pawned jewelry, The Keeper was sure Collins was a worthwhile target. He was guilty. He got away with it and he shouldn't have.

Sandy agreed.

So he sat in his Mazda, sipping his diet Coke, watching. All around him, downtown Spokane bustled with car and foot traffic. Saturday night here was like Saturday night everywhere. Plenty of people were out, drinking and hoping to get lucky. They glided past Sandy in his car, most of them not even noticing him through the slightly tinted windows.

Midnight came and went. Sandy celebrated by eating a Snicker's bar and a banana. He stuffed the wrapper and the peel into his plastic garbage bag while keeping his eyes fixed on the bar door up the street.

At one-oh-five, he was rewarded for his patience. Troy Collins stumbled out of bar and to his truck. Sandy watched him make his way to the truck door, gauging how drunk he might be. He wanted him impaired but not too drunk. A little drunk took away any physical or mental advantage Troy might have. Too much drunk kept the man from feeling any fear.

Collins climbed into the truck, started it up, revved the engine three times and then roasted the tires as he pulled away from the curb.

"Don't call so much attention to yourself," Sandy muttered. "I don't want you getting grabbed up for a deuce tonight."

That would be just his luck. The perfect night to close out this case, except for the happy asshole of a target is driving a huge orange truck with big tires. What were the chances a patrol cop would spot him driving like an idiot, pull him over and hook him up for driving under the influence?

The odds were pretty good, Sandy thought. But he didn't think it was going to happen. Tonight felt lucky.

It didn't take long to figure out that Collins was heading home. The local ladies must have been immune to his charms, Sandy thought. He followed the garish truck up Monroe, across the bridge that traversed the Spokane River and out of the downtown area. Collins drove north until he reached Chelan Avenue, where the neighborhood turned residential.

Sandy drove past Chelan, up a block and circled around.

He knew which house belonged to Collins. It was one of only two on the block that looked like a dump. Most of the others were kept up with well-manicured lawns and decent folk. He guessed the other dive was a rental, but his records showed that Collins owned his home. He'd inherited it from his mother when she died three years ago, and she'd owned it free and clear.

Sandy parked on Lincoln, just around the corner from Chelan. He waited. He'd let Collins get inside. If the man's habits held, he'd stagger into the kitchen for another beer, then flop onto the couch to watch television. Sandy wasn't sure what he watched but he guessed it wasn't anything on the History Channel.

If Collins was too drunk, he'd stagger into the bedroom and go straight to bed. Other than being too hammered from drinking, he really didn't have any other reason to crash, since he didn't have a job to go to in the morning.

If he went to bed, he was too drunk.

But if he watched television…

Sandy waited patiently for fifteen minutes. Once the time had passed, he checked to make sure his dome light was turned off, then exited the car. He tucked his 1911 .45 ACP Peacemaker into his belt. From behind the driver's seat, he removed a small cloth bag containing everything he needed for the job.

Walking halfway up the street and turning down the alley, Sandy maintained a casual pace. It wasn't commonplace for someone to be walking around this late at night, but it wasn't such a strange thing that he expected anyone to call the police about it. Particularly if the person walking around didn't seem suspicious. So Sandy didn't sneak or creep or try not to be seen. He just walked.

The backyard of Collins' house didn't have a gate or a fence. The neighbors on both sides had six foot fences, though. Sandy figured that was to separate themselves from

Collins. He couldn't say he blamed them.

There was no dog to worry about. He didn't figure Collins was responsible enough for a pet. There was only some miscellaneous junk scattered around the long grass. Sandy wended his way through the yard and to the back door. He could see a flickering light through the kitchen window to the left of the door and the muted sound of the television told him everything he needed to know.

Collins was *not* too drunk.

Tonight was lucky.

Sandy stopped at the door. He'd come by earlier, just after dark, and used his lock pick to pop open the lock. Unless Collins was diligent about home security, it should still be unlocked.

He grasped it with his left hand and turned gently. The knob twisted easily in his grip. He eased the door forward. The noise from the television increased in volume. He slipped inside and closed the door behind himself.

The sound of a laugh track from whatever sitcom Collins was watching filled the quiet house. Sandy listened carefully while he withdrew a suppressor from his bag and screwed it onto his .45. He heard no movement upstairs or anywhere else in the house. Collins was alone.

His .45 in one hand and his bag in the other, Sandy walked slowly through the kitchen and toward the living room. He timed his steps to the outbursts of canned laughter from the television. When he reached the doorway of the living room, he took stock of the situation. The front curtains were drawn. He could see the front door from where he stood and it was closed. Collins sat on the couch, staring at the TV like a zombie, absently rubbing his crotch.

Sandy stepped into the room and leveled the .45 at Collins.

Collins detected the movement and turned to look. When

he saw the gun pointed at him, his jaw dropped in surprise and horror. The can of Keystone Light slipped from his fingers. It bounced off the small coffee table and fell to the carpet, where liquid gushed out in a foam. He started making grunting noises. Sandy knew from experience that after about five of those, most people found their voice and started screaming.

"Shut the fuck up," he said in low, powerful tones. "If you start screaming, then I will put a bullet in your skull. You hear me?"

Almost comically, Collins' mouth flapped shut.

Definitely not too drunk, Sandy thought.

"Good," Sandy said. "Now, I want you to listen carefully to me, Troy. If you do that, you just might live tonight. How's that sound?"

Collins nodded furiously.

"Good," Sandy repeated. "Here's how it is going to work. I know you took some jewelry from a woman named Margaret Thompson almost a year ago."

Collins started to shake his head in denial, but Sandy cut him off.

"Don't waste time lying to me, Troy. You and I both know it happened. I'm not the cops, so I don't have to worry about proving it. If you lie to me, I'll just shoot you in the liver. You won't die right away, but you'll eventually bleed out and it won't matter if they send an ambulance and run you to the emergency room." Sandy waggled the .45. "You ever see what one of these can do to a liver? It rips it to shreds. Nothing a doctor can do."

Troy Collins stopped shaking his head. His face seemed a shade whiter to Sandy than before he'd stepped into the room.

"Now, I know you still have some of the jewelry left. I've come to get it for Mrs. Thompson. Where is it?"

Collins paused. Sandy stepped forward and angled the gun toward his mid-section.

"Okay, okay!" shouted Collins.

"Quietly," Sandy growled at him.

"Okay," Collins whispered. "It's in the bathroom. There's a loose tile in the corner by the bathtub. I keep some stuff in there. There might be some of hers left."

"Up," Sandy said.

"Huh?"

"Up," he ordered a second time. "To the bathroom."

Collins rose slowly. Some of the fear and surprise had begun to leave his eyes. Sandy noticed the change. He thought about it for a moment, then made his decision.

"Never mind," he said. "Sit back down."

Collins shrugged and lowered himself back onto the couch. "Look," he started to say.

"No," Sandy said, "you need to listen to me. I'm going to tell you how it's going to be." He reached into his bag and removed a slender bladed hunting knife. He placed it on the table in front of Collins.

"What's that?" Collins asked.

"A knife," Sandy said matter-of-factly. "More accurately, it is a Spencer brand hunting knife. What you're going to do is pick up that knife. You're going to take it firmly in your right hand, insert it into your left wrist and pull it towards you."

"What?"

"Don't cut across the wrist," Sandy instructed. "Cut laterally. The deeper the cut, the faster you'll bleed out."

Collins shook his head. "No fucking way."

"Yes fucking way."

"You're crazy."

"Maybe," Sandy said, "but I'm the one with a .45 pointed at you right now. And if you don't do as I ask, things are going to get messy. I'm talking about kneecaps getting blown apart. I'm talking about groin shots. I'm talking about slow, painful bleed-outs."

Collins made small shakes with his head, stammering. "N-n-no…"

"You are dead either way, Troy," Sandy said coldly. "The knife makes for a relatively painless exit. It hurts a little when you make the cut, but then you just get tired and sleepy and you pass out. That's the easy way." He waggled the gun again. "The hard way is much…well, it's much harder. Lots of pain."

"Please," Collins said, his voice breaking. "I don't want to die."

Sandy felt a small surge of gratitude. Collins wasn't arguing anymore. Just begging. And once the begging began, surrender wasn't far behind.

"I'll do anything you want," Collins sobbed. "I'll give you all my money. Everything."

"I don't want anything from you, Troy," Sandy said. "I just want you to pick up that knife and take care of business."

"Why?" Collins asked, sobbing out the word.

There was a time when Sandy would have answered that question. He thought that even a condemned man deserved an explanation. But after a while, he learned that all it did was delay matters. They knew why. They all knew.

"The knife," Sandy repeated. "Or I go to work with Sam Colt here."

Collins searched out his face, looking for mercy or a lack of conviction. He found neither one. Reluctantly, he reached out for the knife. He stared at it for a long moment. Sandy waited patiently. Finally, Collins moved the blade over until the tip was poised over his left wrist.

Moment of truth, Sandy thought. Which way will he go?

For a second, Sandy thought that Collins might make it easy for him. That he might actually plunge that blade into his own wrist and jerk it back like a samurai committing seppuku over a matter of some dishonor. If he did that, he would bleed out in just a few minutes. When the police eventually came, maybe days from now, they'd find a grisly suicide.

But it was not to be.

Sandy saw the decision in Collins' face, probably before the drunk man even realized he'd made it. He rose from the couch, cocking the knife back and stepping toward Sandy.

Sandy fired twice. The gun gave out a muffled bark, punctuated by the clacking sound of the slide. The bullets slammed into Collins' chest, driving him backward. He flopped onto the couch, staring at Sandy in surprise. His mouth hung open but no sound came out.

Without hesitation, Sandy raised the gun and fired a third shot. It struck Collins in the forehead and shut out his lights forever.

Sandy transitioned immediately to cleanup. First he retrieved the three casings that his gun had ejected. He dropped them into his bag. Then he took the knife from Collins and dropped it in the bag as well. Lastly, he removed a small plastic baggie from his bag. A white powder substance filled one tiny corner of the baggie. He tore a hole in it and sprinkled the methamphetamine on the coffee table.

It wasn't the greatest staging he'd ever done, but the less elaborate something was, the fewer things that could go wrong. Right now, most homicide detectives would survey the scene and figure that poor Troy Collins got robbed of his meth stash. It happens every day in the big, bad city. Especially when you run with bad people.

Sandy found the bathroom. He checked around the bathtub for loose tiles. The second one he tried moved. He lifted the tile and pulled the bag out from inside the hole. The bag had about a dozen different pieces of jewelry. Sandy went through the list of stolen jewelry from the police report in his mind as he perused the contents of the bag. The only item that he was sure belonged to Thompson was a thin gold ring with a small red ruby. He took it. Then he put the bag back in its secret place. Just for good measure, though, he left the tile a little bit cockeyed.

Maybe the detectives will find it. They'll figure the killer was after dope and missed Collins' little treasure trove. Maybe some people will get their stuff back. Maybe they'll tie Collins to some more of the bad shit he'd done.

Or maybe not. Either way, Sandy was finished here.

Walking just as calmly as he'd approached, he slipped out the back door, through the yard and down the alley. He reached his car without feeling eyes upon him. Without pause, he started the car, drove south on Lincoln past Chelan, down another block, then cut over to Post. Once he hit Post, he turned north and drove in a straight line, listening for sirens.

There were none.

Sandy shrugged. He'd gotten away clean. That meant it might be a while before anyone else learned that justice had been served on Troy Collins.

5

The pounding noise started in Sandy's head. It took a while for him to realize it was coming from his door and not between his temples.

"Just a second," he called from his couch. He swung his legs over the edge and planted them on the floor. His head swam momentarily. His stomach lurched. He took a breath and swallowed.

The pounding continued.

Sandy slid his gun from beneath the cushion and stumbled to his feet. At the door, he avoided looking through the peephole, just in case. Instead, he hid the gun behind the door, angling it directly at where he suspected the noisemaker was standing. Then he jerked the door open about a foot.

Brian Moore stood outside, poised and frozen mid-knock.

"Were you sleeping?" he asked, feigning innocence.

"What do you think?" Sandy said evenly.

Brian gave Sandy a quick once-over. "My guess would be that you fell asleep on your couch after putting away a miniscule, sissy amount of whiskey."

Sandy grunted and turned away from the door, leaving it open for Brian to enter. He strode back to the couch and flopped down onto it.

"Did you have that thing pointed at me from behind the door?" Brian asked.

Sandy glanced down at his right hand, which still held the .45. "No," he told Brian. Then he flicked the safety back on and set the pistol on the coffee table next to an almost full bottle of Wild Turkey.

"Liar," Brian replied. He reached down and picked up the bottle. He gauged how much was missing and cast an appraising eye toward Sandy. "You're such a lightweight, Banks. You always were."

"I should be an alcoholic?"

Brian shrugged. "A lot of cops are."

"I'm not a cop anymore. Haven't been for a long time."

"True," Brian said. He settled into the only other place to sit in the living room, a rocking chair made of dark wood. He looked at Sandy and waited.

Sandy returned his look, saying nothing. After a few moments of silence, Brian finally asked, "You finished with your fishing trip?"

"I am," Sandy replied.

"Thus the whiskey," Brian added.

It was Sandy's turn to shrug. He didn't ask Brian how he coped or if he even needed to, so he didn't feel the need to explain himself to the younger man. Maybe Brian enjoyed what they did. Maybe all three of the other Horsemen had. Or maybe, like Sandy, they understood the difference between enjoyment and righteous satisfaction.

Brian grinned and shook his head slightly. "Fishing trip. What a crafty little code, huh? Remember when it was necessary to have some kind of cover story for what we do? How Hank and Bill had to lie to their wives about some bullshit fishing trip to Michigan or Wisconsin or wherever?"

"Minnesota," Sandy corrected. He stifled a yawn.

"Yeah, Minnesota, that's it." He shook his head again. "I even used that line on Paula a couple of times. I guess I wasn't as good at lying as the rest of you, because she figured out I didn't go fishing. You know what she did? I ever tell you about that?"

"No." Sandy rose from the couch and went to the kitchen for some water.

Brian stayed put, raising his voice slightly. "She put a pair of her panties in my tackle box. She used them to wrap up a sexy note about what she was going to do to me when I got home."

"Devious," Sandy said, filling a glass and taking a drink. He started to scrounge around the cupboard for some aspirin.

"Yeah," Brian said. "Except that when I got home and didn't say anything about the nasty things in the note, she got suspicious. All it took was one look in the tackle box to verify things and that was that."

"Huh," Sandy grunted, wondering why in the hell Brian was so chatty today. He never lacked for conversation, but usually became more talkative when he was nervous about something.

"I tried lying to her about it," Brian went on, "but she knew I was lying. Of course, she figured I was cheating on her. I told her I wasn't, which was true, but it's not like I could tell her what I *was* off doing, right?"

"Uh-huh," Sandy said.

"Uh-huh?" Brian asked. "Are you even listening to me?"

"Unfortunately," Sandy answered. He found some Tylenol and popped three in his mouth, washing them down with tap water.

"I'm trying to talk to you, man," Brian said. He sounded strange to Sandy, like he was irritated but also like there was something else going on.

Sandy took another deep breath and let it out. He wasn't really in the mood to play therapist to Brian. "I'm not feeling too talkative this morning."

Brian glanced at his watch. "It's one-thirty, man. It's afternoon."

"Then I'm not feeling too talkative this afternoon."

Brian sighed. "You're a strange dude, Sandy. You always were."

"Strange is a relative term," Sandy replied. He wandered into the living room again and sat back down on the couch. He sipped his water and eyed Brian carefully. "What's up with you?"

"What do you mean?"

"You're acting weird."

"No, I'm not."

Sandy nodded. "Yeah, you are. And I'm asking you what's up?"

Brian opened his mouth, then closed it again without saying anything. He turned and stared at the old-style world map Sandy had framed on the wall.

Sandy waited. He tried to put his finger on Brian's jumpiness, but he couldn't. He felt a strange twinge of suspicion.

"I guess," Brian said after a while, "I'm just feeling kinda nostalgic, you know?"

"No," Sandy said matter-of-factly. "I don't."

Brian dropped his eyes from the picture on the wall and met Sandy's gaze. "I mean, there used to be four of us, right? The Four Horsemen. Like in the Apocalypse. You remember that? Remember when we worked as a team? None of this solo shit."

Sandy said nothing. He twirled his index finger, urging Brian to get to the point.

"We did some great work, huh?" Brian said. "Nailing those scumbags who slipped through the system? What we did, it was what needed to be done. Don't you think so?"

"What's your point?" Sandy asked. He wondered if maybe the problem was that Brian wasn't as okay with things as he had always assumed he was. Maybe he was having a crisis of conscience all at once instead of in little bite-sized pieces like Sandy did every time he finished a job.

"My point?" Brian asked, his face turning harder. "My point, Sandy? My fucking *point* is that we killed a lot of people, okay? Are you saying you're all right with that?"

Sandy didn't reply right away. Then he shrugged. "This is your confessional. Say what you want if it makes you feel any better."

Brian inhaled deeply, then let out a long shuddering breath. His anger seemed to dissipate almost at once. His expression grew wistful. "I don't know if I can feel any better. Hell, part of the reason I feel like shit is because I *don't* feel bad about some of the guys we took out."

Sandy nodded. *That* he understood. He took another sip of water.

"Remember what Bill used to say?" Brian asked. "About how we shouldn't have decided to be the Four Horsemen but should've just called ourselves Karma, Incorporated?"

Sandy felt a slight smile tug at the corner of his mouth. Bill had been a funny guy at times.

Brian leaned back and looked up at the ceiling. "He used to say that karma was a real thing in this world. No, in this *universe*. He said that what goes around, comes around." He smiled. "Then he would always add that, for some people, sometimes you had to be the one to bring it around."

He chuckled, shaking his head.

Sandy wondered briefly if Brian had been drinking himself. He hadn't detected the odor of booze when he answered the door, but he'd been half asleep.

"You drunk?" he asked Brian.

Brian looked at him without leaning forward, drooping his eyelids to do so. "Me? Nah. Just...thoughtful, like I said. I miss Bill, may he rest in peace." He crossed himself sloppily, shaking his head. "Dying of a heart attack just four years after retiring off the job. It's a shame. No other word for it. Just a shame."

Sandy raised his glass in silent tribute, but didn't drink.

"Then we lose Hank," Brian said, staring up at the ceiling again. "Funny, the way that went. He leaves our merry little band of assassins for a woman. He told me he was just tired of lying to her. After what happened between me and Paula, her deciding to call it quits, I found Hank's decision to be kinda ironic, don't you think?"

"The world is full of irony."

"Where'd he head off to?" Brian asked. "Do you know? He never said."

Sandy shrugged. "No one knows."

The twinge of suspicion he'd felt earlier began to grow just a little. Something wasn't right. As the sleep cleared from his mind and the Tylenol began to kick in, his instincts started chiming louder and louder.

Something was up.

"You know who I miss most, though?" Brian asked.

Sandy shook his head.

"Cal," Brian said. "I miss Cal. He was more than just the Keeper. He was the core of it all, don't you think?"

"Cal was a good man," Sandy agreed, his voice almost reverent.

"He was more than that," Brian said. "He was our moral compass. He was the one who made all of this craziness make some kind of sense, much less the guy who made sure the mechanics of it all worked out. When he died…" Brian trailed off, shaking his head. "I don't know. Something changed."

"Everything changes," Sandy said. "That's life."

"Yeah, but it made more sense to me when I knew it was Cal pulling the strings. After he was gone, it started to seem a little wrong somehow." Brian was quiet for a few moments.

Then he asked, "Who do you think he made the Keeper after he left?"

Sandy shrugged.

"No idea?" Brian asked.

"Nope."

"You ever wonder?"

"Nope," Sandy lied.

Brian pursed his lips and shook his head. "I wonder about it. But I figure it'd be the last person any of us would ever suspect. Cal was a crafty old bastard. He wouldn't have made it obvious."

"Cal was smart," Sandy agreed.

"Yeah," Brian said. "Smart." After a few moments, he went on, his voice thick with nostalgia, "We've had a run, huh, Sandy? Just the four of us coming off the job all at once, full of piss and vinegar to set the world right. And if we couldn't do it within the rules, well then to hell with the rules, right? We'd get the job done because it was right, even if it wasn't legal." He cast another glance at Sandy. "Even if it was, basically, you know...murder."

Sandy didn't answer.

Brian seemed not to notice. "I was never much of a religious man, but jee-zus, Sandy. Thou shalt not kill? That's kind of a biggie in most religions."

"Thou shalt not murder," Sandy said quietly.

"Huh?"

"The commandment is 'thou shalt not murder.' Not kill. Murder." Sandy gave him a hard look. "And a righteous kill is not a murder."

"Funny how we can talk ourselves into that, isn't it?" Brian asked. He shook his head, a strange mixture of disgust and nostalgia in his expression. "Why did we do it, Sandy?" he asked. "Why do you think?"

We all have our demons, Sandy thought. And our demons

become our reasons.

The battered, frightened face of a woman flashed in his mind. Her frightened eyes. He pushed the thought away, but another replaced it. This one was kinder, but his memory was fuzzy around the edges.

His mother.

Sandy gave his head a small shake. Goddamn Brian and his nostalgia. He didn't need it. He opened his mouth to say so, then noticed the manila envelope in Brian's hand. Instead of answering, he pointed and asked, "What's that?"

Brian roused himself and looked down at the envelope as if seeing it for the first time. Then he said, "It's a job."

Sandy gave him a puzzled look.

Brian watched him carefully. Then he waved the envelope in the air. "Yeah, I know it's against the rules, bringing it here."

"So why do it?"

Brian didn't reply right away. Finally, he simply shrugged the question away. "It's a goat rope," he told him instead.

"Yeah?"

Brian nodded. "Yeah. You remember Detective Randall Cooper?"

Sandy thought for a moment. A picture of the hulking, lumpy detective formed in his mind. "Yeah, I think so. Not the sharpest crayon in the box, if I remember."

"That's no shit. He was always messing up one little thing or another. Couldn't keep his paperwork straight, missed his deadlines for filing return of service on his warrants, kept evidence in his desk instead of putting it on the books, all those kinds of things. Still," Brian said, smiling slightly, "Coop always did have his head on straight when it came to the facts of his cases. He knew who was lying and who was guilty. Son of a bitch solved cases."

Sandy shook his head. "He didn't solve cases. He figured

out what happened and who did it. That's not solving the case. Solving the case is putting together something that the prosecutor can win at trial."

Brian's smile faded into a small scowl. "Come on, man. I'm not talking about perfect police work here. I'm just saying that the man always had a keen sense of justice."

"Most people outside of the legal profession do," Sandy said wryly.

"*Touché*," Brian allowed. "Anyway, this case is one he bungled up pretty good. He doesn't qualify his informant for the PC for his warrant. Then the warrant itself is weak. It sounds like he denied the guy his lawyer for a while and may have even tuned him up in the interrogation room a bit."

"Good police work for the 1930s, sounds like."

"The problem is still the same," Brian argued. "Whether the cop makes it easy for the judge or not, the situation is that a very guilty piece of shit bad guy got off scot free."

"Why are you telling me about this?" Sandy asked.

Brian leaned forward and dropped the file on the table next to Sandy's .45. "Because it's yours. The retainer is still in there."

"Mine?"

"Yours."

Sandy shook his head. "Uh-uh. You catch it, you clean it."

"Ah, yes," Brian chuckled without any humor in the sound. "The mantra of the Four Horsemen."

He glanced at the file and the .45 next to it. Then he looked up at Brian. "I suppose this is a good time to ask you again – what is going on with you?"

Something flickered behind Brian's eyes. It disappeared before Sandy could get a read on it, replaced by obvious weariness. Brian sighed. "I'm done, Sandy. I'm out."

"The hell you say."

"No," Brian said. "Really. I can't do this anymore. I

can't…I can't keep it at an arm's length like I used to be able to."

"You're serious."

Brian nodded. "One hundred percent. It's either that or start drinking more. Or doping. Or something. Because the dreams are starting to catch up to me." He paused and swallowed. "Just about every night, actually."

Sandy didn't reply. He had the dreams, too. Sometimes he had dreams about a job going sideways. His gun wouldn't work, or the guy would be too lightning fast for him to handle. In those dreams, he always failed somehow and usually woke up as he was being killed. Other times, though, he dreamt about what he actually did. He relived every vivid detail of what really happened on the jobs he'd completed. The truth was, he couldn't say which dreams were worse.

"So," Brian said, "I'm done. I don't have some girl that I'm tired of lying to like Hank did. And I don't want to hide behind dope or drink or wait until I die of a heart attack like what happened to Bill. I'm just going to leave while I have some piece of my soul intact."

Sandy raised his eyebrows slightly at Brian's words. They were more poetic than he was used to from the short, swarthy man. Brian's usual idea of elegant poetry was a limerick with a double entendre.

"That means I can't do this last job," Brian said. "I know I'm violating more than a couple of our precious rules by bringing it here, but I couldn't wait. I saw it in the mail slot earlier this week, and I just…" he struggled for words, then shrugged. "I was just done."

Sandy sat quietly, considering Brian's words. The discomfort or nervousness he'd noticed earlier was starting to make sense to him now.

Brian waited a few seconds, then asked him, "Will you do this for me, Sandy? Will you take this job?"

Sandy looked down at the manila folder on the table, then back to Brian. The news that he was losing his last partner hadn't sunk in yet. He had no idea what he would do with this job or any other.

"I'll look at it," he finally answered.

"Good enough," Brian said. "I can't ask for more."

Brian rose from his seat and held out his right hand. Tears formed in his eyes. He brushed them away irritably with his left hand.

"Sorry, Sandy," he said. "I hate doing this to you. I just don't feel like I have a choice anymore."

Sandy stood and took Brian's hand. The smaller man's palm was clammy with sweat, but he gripped Sandy's hand in a firm handshake.

"There's an old saying," Sandy said, "that a man's gotta do what a man's gotta do."

Brian smiled through his tears. "What's that, some John Wayne wisdom or something?"

Sandy shrugged. "I just heard it somewhere. Call it common wisdom."

"Well, thanks either way," Brian said, pumping Sandy's hand one final time and letting go. "I appreciate you making this easier for me. I have to tell you, I was scared as hell to come here today. I didn't want to do this to you…you know, tell you."

"I could tell," Sandy said.

"I'm sure. I was nervous. I felt like I was letting you down somehow."

Sandy shook his head. "We had a good run. You stood tall. You're not letting me or anyone else down."

"You mean that, Sandy?" Brian peered at him closely, his tone urgent. "You really mean that?"

"Yeah," Sandy said, assuring him. "I do."

Brian swallowed hard, took another deep breath and let it

out. "All right. Then I'm off. You want to know where to?"

"No," Sandy said. "But I hope you find peace, wherever it is."

Brian's face broke into a grin. "Peace. There's a word I never thought I'd be this in love with."

Peace, Sandy thought. That elusive state that seems to pull further away with every job.

"Good luck, Brian," was all he said.

"Thanks."

Brian turned and made his way to the door. His hand came to rest on the knob. Then he paused. Looking over his shoulder, he asked, "How's it feel?"

"What's that?"

"To be the last one standing. How's that feel?"

Sandy didn't answer right away. Too many thoughts were buzzing through his head. He didn't need to worry about coming up with a reply, though. Brian didn't wait for one. He turned the knob, stepped through the doorway and closed the door behind him without another word.

And just like that, he was the only one left. The last Horseman.

6

Sandy took a shower while the coffee brewed. He stood under the spray of water, twisting the knob until it was as hot as he could stand. The water blasted his skin like bee stings. He focused on the sensation, trying to clear his mind.

When he was finished, he made some toast. Only after he'd poured a cup of the strong, black coffee and chewed several bites of toast did he turn his mind toward what had happened.

Bill was dead.

Hank was long gone.

And now Brian had left.

He was alone.

Now, all of the cases would be his.

He asked himself if he could keep up with it. Was it even logistically possible? With all of the prep work he did and surveillance, could he take on a greater load and still operate efficiently? Most importantly, could he do it without arousing undue suspicion or getting caught?

Sandy took a bite of his toast and chewed. He stared out the small window off the back of his apartment. He let the numbers roll around in his head, calculating as reasonably as possible without putting pen to paper.

He swallowed.

Probably.

He could *probably* still make it work.

But it would be a full time job. And his risk would go up. Of course, so would the pay, such as it was.

Sandy took another bite. He chewed for a little while, then swallowed and chased the toast with a long sip of his coffee. He knew that the real question wasn't if he *could* go on, but rather if he *wanted* to.

For this one, he didn't listen to his head. The message from that portion of his being was jumbled enough as it was. Some parts clamored for finishing a job, others argued that it was a job that would never be done. The question of justice, always a frequent contender, reared up and made an appearance. Logistical and logical concerns battled for a voice, too.

Sandy ignored them all.

He listened to his gut.

"Is it enough?" he asked aloud, looking down into the blackness of his coffee.

Had he done enough to make up for Yvonne Lewis, the battered wife he'd failed? Had he tipped the scales of justice enough times to even that score, to somehow balance that terrible mistake? Could he stand at her graveside now, knowing he'd let her down all those years ago and truly feel redemption?

Maybe. That was the funny thing about guilt and making up for great failures. All those good deeds seemed to weigh little in comparison to what they were making up for. How many bad guys did it take to make up for one battered woman that became a domestic violence homicide victim because of him? Was there even a number?

There probably was. Maybe he'd feel it in his gut when he'd somehow reached that marker. Perhaps the tightness in his chest would go away. The ache in his stomach might fade. Maybe Yvonne Lewis could rest in peace.

Sandy shook his head slowly. Even if that were to come to pass, there was another debt. Another, much older failure.

And this one carried an even higher price tag on it. He didn't think he could ever bring enough justice in the world to make up for *that* one.

So the question wasn't if he'd done enough, or if he *could* ever do enough. The question was—

"Do you want to keep going?" he asked aloud.

The answer was overwhelming and immediate.

No.

He didn't.

He was done. As done as Brian. As done as Hank. If ever they'd accomplished something akin to justice, their time was over now. He could feel it in his bones. The conviction was palpable, irrefutable. At first, he wondered why he hadn't sensed this before today, but he knew the truth. As long as there were two of them, it was a duty.

Now it was just him.

"So I'm done," he murmured. He sipped his coffee again. Some of the hot liquid spilled, splashing on his chin and burning.

He realized it was because he was smiling.

Once the idea sunk in, he went to the junk drawer in the kitchen. He pushed aside a hammer, a few screwdrivers and other odds and ends until he found a notepad. He dug around a little longer until he located a pen. Then he stood at the counter, staring down at the empty page.

A life unlived, he thought.

Was there a piece of it still there, though?

Was that possible?

He lowered the pen to paper, but hesitated. How could he sum everything up in one letter? It seemed that everything since his childhood was threatening to come rumbling out if he started writing now. Just a small bit would not do.

No, he thought. It had to be everything, or nothing.

He started to put the pen down, then hesitated again. Maybe he could write just a little. Just enough.

He didn't allow himself to think about it any longer. Instead, he quickly scratched out the few words that he felt comfortable with.

> *Dear Janet,*
> *I know it's been a long time. I'm sorry for that.*
> *But I think I'll be home soon. I've missed you,*
> *and I love you.*

He didn't bother signing it. She'd know who it was. He tore the page from the pad and folded it into thirds. After scrounging around the apartment for five minutes, he located an envelope. He wrote the address from memory. He provided no return address.

He slipped the envelope into his back pocket, took a deep breath and confronted the file folder on the table.

It would have to go to office. He'd have to see to that. Put it in the desk drawer and call it good.

Sandy slid the .45 into his belt. He put on a light jacket to cover it up. With the file under his arm, he made his way to the car. His steps felt lighter than he could ever remember. He wondered if this was how POWs felt when they were freed.

I've been a POW of sorts, he thought to himself. A prisoner of our secret little war against the system.

As he started the car and headed toward the office, Sandy let that thought linger. He decided that it hadn't been a war exactly. More like a crusade. And then he had to admit that, all things considered, the whole thing was probably not a success.

Did they do any good at all?

Sandy took a deep breath and let it out. The question irritated him. It was one he asked himself after every job. More to the point, he wondered if it was ever right to do evil – because what else would you call murder? – to accomplish a good end.

Maybe it was right that he thought of it as a war. He was pretty sure that these were questions that soldiers asked themselves as every generation had their war. It was an answer that, for a soldier, was much clearer.

At least as far as Sandy was concerned.

He drove silently. He left the radio off. The whine of the engine was the only music he listened to. The houses and businesses flitted by as he headed straight to the office.

The gate to the storage facility was locked. Sandy punched in the security code and it slid open. He drove to the back corner. He parked the car a ways away from the unit. As he walked toward the office, habit drove him to glance around casually to make sure no one was watching. He saw nothing.

At Unit 88, he paused again to look around. When he saw that everything was clear, he worked the combination lock on the roll up door. He spun the digits to 5-2-7 and tugged the lock downward. It snapped open. Sandy removed it and put it in his back pocket. Then he rolled up the door, stepped inside and quickly lowered the door again. He left enough space open at the bottom to let in some light until he found the kerosene lamp and fired it up. Then he shut the door flush and firm to the concrete.

Sandy flopped the file on the desk as he sat down. He reached for the right hand drawer, then paused. After a moment, his hand drifted to the left hand drawer. He pulled it out all the way, exposing a drawer full of files. Almost every one of them had a red X through the name on the tab, signifying a success. A complete success meant making the scene look like something other than what it was. A drug overdose, a suicide, an accident. Anything that didn't arouse suspicion, so those few that were obvious homicides didn't stack up and get attention. The last thing they wanted was someone connecting the dots and deciding that some kind of a serial killer was at work. Sandy was pretty sure that they couldn't have withstood that kind of investigative scrutiny or intense pressure from police resources.

There were a few with green dots. All had a story. In some cases, the targets were simply not found. If they'd left the region long-term, standard practice was to let them be. Of course, if they returned to the Lilac City, then the file went active again. Sandy couldn't think of a time that had happened, but it was nice in theory.

He knew one of the green dots was there because the target had developed pancreatic cancer. The Horseman who had that one – Bill, judging by the handwriting – decided that nature was doling out justice better than he ever could. Besides, it was in keeping with Bill's theory on karma.

Sandy was responsible for one green dot. In the year between his trial and The Keeper sending the file, one of the targets had changed his life around. Sandy didn't know how recent the change was, but after following the man around for three weeks, he was pretty certain it was genuine.

He looked at the full drawer. The tabs stuck up from the files and he ran his fingers over them. He resisted the urge to count how many were in the drawer.

A lot, he thought. A whole fucking lot.

And most of them had red Xs on them.

Sandy closed the drawer. He pulled open the second drawer, extending it out as far as the runners allowed. It was about one-third full. Red Xs stared up at him like the cartoon eyes of a stick figure character that had been killed.

He started to put Brian's file in the back, then stopped.

He should at least label it. As insane as that was, it was no more insane than everything he'd been doing – what all of them had been doing – for the last twelve years. Might as well finish the job.

The middle drawer had a few pens and pads of paper inside. He fished around for a moment until he found a green marker. The cap made a loud plastic pop when he pulled it off. Then he slid the file out of the manila envelope. A stack of wrapped, crisp one hundred dollar bills came with it. He brushed the money aside and sat for a long while, the pen poised over the file tab. He stared at the name.

JEFF ODOMS.

Never heard of him.

Below that, the crime.

KIDNAP/RAPE X 2 – J.

Sandy swallowed. The code was simple. Jeff Odoms was a kidnapper and a rapist. With two victims. And the victims were both juveniles.

"Goddamnit," he muttered.

He capped the pen and set it aside. Then he flipped open the file and began to read.

7

"We should grab him now," she said, fingering the small portable radio as they sat in the sedan.

"I know," he told his partner. "But orders is orders."

"Nice grammar."

"I was being cute."

"No one thinks you're cute."

"My wife thinks I'm cute."

She shook her head. "She may have thought that at one point in time. I think that exit is in the rear-view mirror now."

"Like you would know."

"I know," she said. "I'll tell you what else I know. We should take this guy down now, while we have him hemmed in. It's the smart way to do it."

"You're right," he agreed. He reached up and twisted the car radio knob, changing the station away from a commercial hawking cholesterol reducing medicine to the oldies station. Mitch Ryder came over the speakers. He smiled, but kept the volume low.

She watched him, then said, "We could, you know."

"Could what?"

"Just do it. Arrest him."

He shook his head. "Busting orders is not on my list of smart career moves. I've got kids. And a wife, who may or may not think I'm cute, but to whom I still have an obligation."

She sighed. "Fine. But these orders are wrong."

"Of course they are. Look who gave them."

"True," she conceded. "But what is he looking for? More evidence? The guy is surrounded by twelve years' worth of evidence right now. Which he could be in there burning, for all we know."

"He's not."

"How do you know?"

"You see any smoke?"

"No."

He held his hands up in a 'there you are' gesture.

"What if he was, though?" she asked. "What if he was in there burning up the evidence of a twelve year murder for hire scheme?"

"We'd go in for that. Exigent circumstances."

"Which gives us some discretion."

"Some. We'd still get the fuzzy end of the lollipop when it was all said and done, but I don't think we get bounced over it."

She nodded absently in agreement. After a moment of thought, she said, "You know, he could be using a shredder instead of burning the files."

"Could be."

"So we should –"

"Of course, there's no indication of that, thus no exigency."

She frowned. "So we'll just sit here anyway, because our boss is a moron."

"He's a moron who wants a promotion," he said.

"To what? Head-Dipshit-in-charge?"

"Doesn't matter what you call it when it comes with a pay raise and a cushy office back in D.C.," he told her. "That's why this case will make exactly when and how he decides, based on how big a splash he can make with the operation."

"I hate politics," she muttered.

"Better get used to them," he said. "You won't see retirement if you can't navigate those waters at least a little bit."

"Those waters are full of sewage as far as I'm concerned."

"True." He smiled. "Which is a good reason not to rock the boat too much."

8

Sandy sat parked in his Mazda, sipping diet Coke. He watched the house mid-block. A dark green rancher with glossy white trim, the place had a neatly manicured lawn and a knee-high white picket fence surrounding the front yard.

Someone is trying to keep up appearances, Sandy thought.

He glanced at his watch, which was usually a mistake. Surveillance was long work. It required patience. Clock-watching just made things drag on more slowly and diverted his attention from what he was supposed to be doing.

Ten-thirty-eight. That's what the slightly luminescent green hands on his watch read.

Sandy took another sip of his diet Coke and leaned back. What was Jeff Odoms up to tonight, he wondered. So far, the man seemed to live a structured, boring existence. He worked for a textile company down on Monroe Street. From what Sandy had discovered in his research, the job was probably a solitary one that involved piecing together smaller pieces of fabric into a finished product. Of course, Odoms could be a supervisor or even mid-management. The information Sandy was able to uncover on the Internet only listed the very top echelon of the company.

Somehow, though, Odoms didn't seem like the manager type. He seemed more like the quiet, dependable employee who kept to himself.

Every day after work, Odoms went home. This routine had been interrupted only once and that was for a trip to the grocery store. Once home, Odoms remained there. No trips to the bars. No dates. No buddies over for the Gonzaga basketball game. Just Odoms, all by himself.

Sandy noticed that the light to a front corner room stayed on longer than all the rest. He figured that was where Odoms kept his computer. The light burned well into the night. When it finally went out, the bathroom light and then the bedroom light came on for a short while each before Odoms retired to his slumber.

The light was on right now. Sandy stared at it.

I wonder what he's doing in that office every night? He thought, not for the first time. He imagined Odoms scouring the Internet for images that fed his fetish. Based on what he read in the file about the crimes Odoms had committed, those images were likely violent, degrading and sick.

In short, Jeff Odoms was exactly the kind of criminal that the Four Horseman had been created to deal with. That's why Sandy couldn't simply file the case away after he read it. If he had, he knew that the images of those two fifteen year old girls would haunt him mercilessly for the rest of his life.

He half-considered adding Detective Randall Cooper to the hit list for bungling the case so badly. Had he not misstepped so egregiously, the judge would not have suppressed most of the evidence. With that evidence in play, Sandy doubted any jury would have failed to convict Odoms.

This project wasn't formed to rescue stupid or lazy cops from bad police work, he groused silently. It was created to right grievous wrongs. To set things straight. To give justice a second shot at being served. In Odoms' case, justice should have been rendered the first time around. All the pieces were there. Cooper just flat out fucked up. Repeatedly.

Police work was like every other profession, Sandy knew. You had your hard workers and you had your lazy ones. You had smart, motivated, dedicated cops and then you had some who were just coasting along at the minimum accepted standards.

Like Detective Randall Cooper.

Despite his distaste for Cooper's handling of the case – or his entire existence – Sandy couldn't let Odoms slide. What he did was too horrible. The fact that he got away with it, regardless of the reason, only made it more horrible. As soon as Sandy read the file, he knew that if he had ever believed in what the Horsemen represented, he had to finish this last job. Maybe there would always be another job waiting in the wings that would go undone, but at least he wouldn't know the details of those.

Those victims wouldn't have names.

Like Mariko.

Like Suzume.

The corner light went off. A moment or two later, the small window up high on the side of the house illuminated. Five minutes later, it also went dark. The back corner window lit up behind shades for a few minutes, then became black.

Sandy looked down at his watch. Eleven-oh-four and Mr. Jeff Odoms was tucked away in his bed.

Sandy sat in the car for a while longer, considering. He had his go-bag in the trunk. He could dispense with this job tonight. Finish it. Then he'd be free to move on and leave this life behind. The last Horseman could ride into the sunset.

But he knew that he was forcing the issue. Being too hasty. For one thing, he needed to scout out the back yard again. More importantly, he needed to see if he could prepare the back door for swifter entry.

Not tonight, he decided.

The next morning, he followed Odoms to work. Once his target was inside, Sandy felt comfortable that he'd stay there until the end of his work day. He waited an hour just to be sure, then drove to the post office where the drop box was located.

He figured that the only way to get a message to The Keeper that the project was over would be to close the mailbox. He wasn't even sure if that would work, but he couldn't think of another way.

He wished for the thousandth time that Lieutenant Cal Ridley was still around. He was the original Keeper, the mastermind behind the entire project. He recruited each of the Horsemen. He laid out the ground rules, the safety precautions, all of it. After two years, though, word came that he had been diagnosed with throat cancer. He let the Horsemen know he was dying and that he was passing the torch. What he didn't tell them was who the new Keeper would be.

That was better for everybody, he told them the last time they met. The Keeper didn't know who the Horsemen were and the Horsemen didn't know who the Keeper was. He created a double-blind operation that kept each cell safe if one were compromised.

Sandy had wondered why Ridley hadn't done the same thing with the individual Horsemen, too. Eventually, though, he came to understand. What the Horsemen did was difficult, even if it was righteous. It flew in the face of what they'd learned as cops or even what they'd learned as citizens. It was beyond law. That took a toll on a man. Having some fellowship softened that experience. It gave him a sense of fraternity that counter-balanced the guilt that seeped in.

Seeped? Hell, it flooded in. That's why Hank quit, and now Brian, too. It might have been what gave Bill the heart attack, for all he knew. And the truth was, that was why Sandy was going to call it quits himself.

As soon as he finished with Odoms.

Sandy parked his car in the post office lot. He headed inside. At the window, he bought a single stamp. He walked over to the outgoing mail slot, stuck the stamp on the corner of his letter to Janet and slipped it through.

Good journey, he thought. *See you soon.*

Along one wall, a slew of different forms were available. He searched until he found the one he wanted. Carefully, he filled out the form cancelling the rent on the post office box. On the authorization block, he scrawled an illegible signature that he hoped would pass muster.

He knew he couldn't take the form back to the employee at the window. Instead, he folded it so that the name of the form would be staring the postman in the eye when he delivered mail to the box. Sandy removed the key from his key ring, since he'd need to leave that in the box, too. He used his key to open up the mail slot.

A dark yellow manila envelope filled the small box.

Sandy stared at it for a long while.

Another job.

He wrestled with his thoughts until he realized that he had to take the file. Whether he worked it or not, he had to take it.

Sandy pulled the envelope from the box. He slid the closure form into the box, pressing the stiffly folded upright part against the rear. He weighted it down with the mailbox key.

Then he took a deep breath.

Once he closed the mailbox, he was done. There would be no more jobs. Odoms would be the last. There'd be no more. The Keeper would find this drop box to be a dead end. The Horsemen were finished.

Sandy swung the mailbox shut, closing it with a sharp click. Then he turned and strode out of the post office for the last time.

Back in his car, he tossed the unopened envelope onto the

passenger seat. He started the car and pulled out of the parking lot into traffic. He would have to go to the office to file this case. That would also likely be his final visit. He'd review the Odoms file again while he was there.

Sandy's eyes flicked to the rear view mirror. Out of habit, he continuously scanned his surroundings. He noticed a medium blue sedan, probably a Taurus, two cars back and in the next lane over. Something nagged at him about the car. He knew he'd seen it recently on a couple of occasions. Initially, he thought it was coincidence. He thought he was just seeing a common make, model and color. Of course, once you started noticing a particular type of car, they suddenly appeared everywhere.

But no, this was the same car. He wasn't sure right away how he knew, but he knew it. As he watched the car in his mirrors more closely, the little facts that told him it was the same car started to add up.

The design of the dirt at the edge of the wiper blade's range was the same.

A small, pinpoint dent on the passenger front bumper. Not enough to worry about fixing, but enough to just barely notice.

A slightly bluish tint to the day headlights that indicated a strong Halogen or similar bulb.

And probably the biggest tip-off of all, two people in the front seat. A man and a woman. The woman was driving. They both wore suits, jackets and all.

Sandy clenched his jaw.

Cops.

Had to be.

Not locals, though. City detectives didn't wear suits, except maybe to court. They wore khaki's or slacks and a collared shirt. Maybe a tie, but rarely a jacket. And definitely not while out in the field on some sort of surveillance. In fact, if city cops were following him, he'd expect them to be in jeans and a T-shirt, blending into the local population.

That meant Staties. Or Feds.

A cold sweat broke out all over Sandy's body. Avoiding the police had been second nature for him on this project, but that was mostly restricted to the times when he wrapped up an assignment. That was why he conducted such exhaustive prep work – so that his short, few minutes of exposure went like clockwork.

But this was something different than getting caught in the finishing moments of a job. This was pro-active work, not reactive. It wasn't happenstance, but planned. And that meant something else entirely. Something more dangerous.

Sandy took a deep breath and let it out. He kept driving, maintaining an outwardly calm composure.

"Who the fuck are you guys?" he muttered to himself.

Now that he knew they were there, he had an advantage he didn't have before. He couldn't let them know that he was aware of their presence. If he did, one of two things would happen. If they were prepared to arrest him for something, a blown cover would probably hasten that event. But if they thought their cover was still in place, they might hold off for a while longer. He didn't know how long, but any time at all was a gift right now. It gave him the opportunity to think, to decide on his course of action.

On the other hand, if they weren't ready to arrest him for something, they'd react to the blown cover by setting up new surveillance, which he'd have to spot all over again. Doubtless, it would be better.

No, his best move was to pretend he was unaware of their presence. Take advantage of the time he had. Gather what intel he could from counter-surveillance.

And decide what the hell to do.

Sandy turned right on Indiana instead of left. What he

couldn't do was lead them to the office, just in case they didn't already know about it. They'd seen him go into the post office, that much was already certain. He didn't have the key anymore, so they couldn't link him to the box with that. Of course, the piece of mail sitting on his passenger seat would provide all the connection they needed.

Shit, he thought. Shit, fuck, motherfuck.

If they were on him, they no doubt knew where he lived. He could head there. Take the file inside. Destroy it. Make a plan.

But what if they piled out of the car after he parked and started for the door? Then they'd have him red-handed, with a smoking gun.

And as far as that was concerned, his .45 and the suppressor were hidden in the floor of his bedroom. They may or may not find it in a search, but if they did and they knew which cases to link it to, he was screwed. Done like dinner. They'd do a ballistic match and it'd be a slam dunk. Even a mope like Randall Cooper couldn't make enough mistakes to blow that case. And he doubted that the likes of Randall Cooper were in the car that was following him.

Then again, their surveillance techniques weren't the greatest. A real surveillance job would be more coordinated and involve several cars, both ahead and behind the target. So maybe this was a fishing expedition of some kind, to find out about him.

Or maybe they were just the lead car and this was an arrest operation.

An arrest operation organized by who? Feds? State Patrol? And how much did they know?

Sandy's mind whirred. This was the first time in twelve years that he'd been followed. That alone was unsettling. Beyond that, there were too many questions. Too many unknowns.

He had to make a decision.

Take a chance and play out the string.

Sandy cursed under his breath. Could he afford to risk going home?

No. He was on the second floor. If he went inside his apartment and they decided to move on him, he'd be trapped with no escape route except shooting his way out. And that was a losing proposition.

He had to slip surveillance. Then he had to get rid of this new file. After that he could figure out who the hell was following him and what he was going to do next.

His heart thudded in his ears. He wiped his sweaty hands on his jeans, then turned on the radio and adjusted the station. J. Geils came on, singing about his angel in the magazine centerfold. Sandy barely heard the words. He watched the flow of traffic carefully. At every intersection, he looked for the opportunity to time the light so that he made it through the yellow and his trail car caught the red. He knew that if they broke the red to come after him, all bets were off and they were set to arrest him. If they waited, he had a little breathing room.

At Monroe, he got his chance. Indiana ran into Northwest Boulevard here, turning sharply to the northwest for the arterial. The light turned yellow as he was two car lengths away. He held his speed, trying to appear as if he were casually going through the intersection. There was no need to hurry. The light turned red when he was mid-way through the intersection. He looked in his rear-view mirror. The blue Taurus was caught behind a green Volvo that had stopped for the light.

He continued along Northwest Boulevard, watching carefully. The Taurus made no effort to get around the Volvo or chase after him.

He breathed a sigh of relief. They were a soft tail.

Good.

He sped up slightly, but stayed in the left lane until he

knew that he was far enough away to be out of view from the intersection behind him. Then he switched into the right-hand lane. He caught the red at Maple, but he was first in line so he made a quick right hand turn onto the northbound arterial. He kept his speed with the flow of traffic, watching his rear view mirror. There was no sign of the Taurus.

At Garland, he turned left. He drove the eight blocks or so to Belt, still watching for any tail.

He saw none.

At Belt, he turned north. He made his way almost to Wellesley, then turned into the large shopping center that ran from Belt clear over to Alberta. He was in the midst of a huge Wal-Mart lot, complemented by hardware stores, a strip containing a bank, a Starbucks, a liquor store and a Safeway grocery store.

Sandy found an empty parking stall and stopped. He sat there for fifteen minutes, carefully scanning the area for any surveillance units. He saw nothing suspicious. He stepped outside his car and searched the sky for air coverage. If this was a big enough operation, a helicopter wasn't out of the question. He saw a commercial plane flying low toward the airport and a jet of some kind in the distance, but nothing that raised any suspicion.

Feeling a little safer, he turned to his car. He searched the wheel wells and under the body of the car for any sort of GPS device. He knew that the transmitters today were small, even tiny, so he carefully combed the underside of his Mazda.

A pair of footsteps approached. Sandy expected them to pass by, as several shoppers already had. These didn't. A pair of glossy wing-tip dress shoes stopped a few feet away from him.

"Car trouble?" came a male voice.

Sandy tensed. This could be it. Maybe their surveillance had been better than he thought. Or maybe there was a GPS unit and he just hadn't found it yet. He'd been there long enough for them to regroup and send in the troops.

"Just looking for a leak," Sandy said, keeping his voice even.

He slid out from under the car.

The man stood near the rear of Sandy's Mazda. He looked about forty. His blond hair was short, reminding Sandy of how a banker would wear it. Or a cop. He wore a casual polo shirt and slacks. No gun or badge. The only thing on his belt was a PDA in a square holster. Both hands held plastic Wal-Mart bags.

"All right," the man said with a shrug. "Just thought I'd check."

"Thanks," Sandy answered. "That was nice of you."

The man smiled. The short scar that ran from the bottom of his lip toward his chin stretched when he did so. "I've been stuck with car trouble before. Sucks to have to call Triple-A."

Sandy didn't reply.

"Then again, that's why you pay the premiums, isn't it? For when you need them."

Sandy nodded, his expression non-committal.

The man returned the nod, turned and walked away. Sandy popped open his hood and pretended to inspect the motor briefly while he watched the man go. When he got into a small convertible BMW, he breathed a sigh of relief. No cop drove a Beemer on duty. Not even undercover. Not even the Feds.

In fact, *especially* not the Feds.

He dropped the hood into place. Then he opened the passenger door, removed the file and headed toward the business strip. He resisted the urge to go into the liquor store and get a bottle of something to steady his nerves. Instead, he went into the coffee shop.

Once he had a cup of decaf, he settled into a corner table.

He turned the envelope with the address face-down and let his mind set to work on the problem.

9

"You *lost* him?" The voice on the telephone was not pleased.

"Yeah." His reply was sheepish. He glanced at his partner. She gave him an inquisitive look in return.

"How did *that* happen?"

"It wasn't Lori's fault. It was the timing of the traffic lights, that's all."

"You lost the target and now you're going to sell me some happy bullshit about traffic lights?"

"It's true. He buzzed through a yellow and the car in front of us stopped for the red."

"Did he make you?"

"I don't think so. He didn't speed up or anything. He just caught the light perfectly."

"And you let him go?"

"Well, sir, we could've broke the light, probably, but that would've blown our cover. If we did that, then – "

"I don't need an education on our strategy, Special Agent."

"No, sir."

"What I need is for you to stay on this subject like a second skin."

"Yes, sir."

"You need to be between him and his shadow, that's how close I want you."

"Yes, sir. We were, but then – "

"And I'm not interested in any excuses. Get me?"

He fell silent. Then, "Yes, sir. I understand." He glanced over at Lori. "*We* understand."

"Good. Now what's your plan?"

"We're going to check around some large public areas. The mall, shopping centers, areas like that. If we don't pick him up in the next couple of hours, we'll sit off his apartment and try to reacquire him there."

"Change cars before you do that. He may have just caught the light like you said, but it's a little suspicious that you couldn't catch up to him again after that. Get a new car before you set up on his house, just in case."

"Yes, sir."

"Good."

"Uh, sir…?"

"Go ahead."

"If it turns out that he is aware of our surveillance, shouldn't we just make our move and arrest him? I mean, we already have everything from the CI—"

"That's my call, Special Agent, not yours. I'm the Agent-in-Charge. This operation is nearing completion, but I'll decide when it is time to lower the boom on this guy. Meanwhile, I don't want him to get a sniff of us and slip away. So do your job."

"Yes, sir."

The line went dead without a reply.

He looked over at his partner and shrugged. "Sorry," he said.

"Thanks for trying," Lori told him.

"No problem." He shook his head in mild amazement. "How in the hell did that guy ever get to be a boss? He's such an uptight asshole."

"That is exactly how he got to be a boss," Lori said. She

turned the ignition key and started the Taurus. "Let's hit the Northtown Mall parking lot first."

10

Sandy sat in the corner of the coffee shop with his back against the wall. He slowly spun the half-empty coffee cup on its base, listening to the paper scrape against the Formica tabletop. He stared absently toward the front door, examining each new customer that walked in. None aroused his suspicion.

He glanced down at the still unopened manila envelope. Inside was a file probably every bit as heinous as the Odoms file. Some bad guy that got away with something horrible. Someone who wouldn't know justice unless it came at his hand.

No, he decided. He couldn't be responsible any more. He did his time. His duty. All of them had. It was time for it to end.

And none too soon, since it was clear that some branch of law enforcement was looking at him.

Sandy focused on his next move. Assuming that the cops who had been following him were state, or more likely, federal, where did that leave him? He had to dump this file and disappear. It was that simple. Do not go home. Do not pass Go. Do not collect on the misdeeds of Odoms or whatever sick bastard was inside the sealed file next to him.

If the feds were on to him, though, then they were probably onto the whole operation. That meant Brian and Hank were at risk. And The Keeper.

Hank had slipped away years ago. No one knew where to, and Sandy imagined that it was likely to stay that way. If the feds located him, he'd have to work that out on his own. Sandy had no way to warn him.

Brian might still be accessible, though. Sandy knew where he lived. Brian may have already left the area, too, but if not, the least Sandy could do was go over to his house and warn him. He didn't expect he'd still be there, though. If it had been Sandy checking out, he'd have made all of his preparations before he ever came to see the last Horseman. After that final conversation, he'd have disappeared.

Still, he owed Brian a warning.

The Keeper, too.

Sandy frowned. That one was more problematic. How could he warn someone that he had no line of communication with? Someone whose identity he didn't know?

He tried to remember all of the names of the cops he'd worked with a dozen years ago. Who among them would Lieutenant Cal Ridley entrust with knowledge of the Four Horsemen? Who would be at ease not only with the reason for their existence, but with the logistical details as well? The slush fund, for example, that Ridley used to funnel money their way for operational needs? Who would be smart enough to pick only the most righteous of cases for them to work? To do the follow-up before placing the file in the drop box?

To not get caught.

Sandy could think of no one. Truth be told, the faces and names of those long ago people were hazy memories now. He wasn't going to figure out who The Keeper was by going down Memory Lane.

Besides, Ridley wouldn't have picked someone obvious.

He was too devious for that. Too detail-oriented. He'd have picked someone that none of them would be able to figure out. He knew that they'd try, if for no other reason than to satisfy the driving curiosity that was an undeniable part of their makeup. That curiosity was the reason most of them became cops to begin with.

Ridley had been right in that respect. More than once, the four of them sat in the office, drinking beer and theorizing about the identity of the new Keeper. But it had been all talk. No one had a clue. No one ever came up with anything other than speculation, either.

The truth was, until today, it didn't really matter. The operation hadn't faltered after Ridley passed away. The files kept coming. The targets were good ones. The Horsemen did their part, first as a group. Then, as Bill left, then Hank, their operations devolved into solo operations.

Sandy raised the cup to his lips and sipped. His coffee was lukewarm. He felt a duty to warn The Keeper, but how? He couldn't risk going back to the mail drop. Even if the cops or the feds or whoever it was hadn't known about it before, they'd been following him. Unfortunately, he'd led them there himself. It was no longer safe.

So how? How to contact someone he'd never met and didn't know when the only line of communication has been severed?

How?

Sandy clenched his jaw slightly. He squinted down at the splash of coffee left in his cup. Then his mind caught on something. A possibility. He paused for a moment and considered.

Would she know anything?

Maybe, he thought.

Sandy rose from his seat, tossed the half-empty cup into the trash and headed out to his car.

"Banks, you say?" she asked him through the screen door.

"Yes, ma'am. Sandy Banks. I worked with your husband, years ago."

A smile crossed her lips. "You knew my Cal?"

"I did."

"And you're a policeman?"

Sandy shook his head. "Not anymore. I'm retired."

Gail Ridley unlocked the screen door and pushed it open. "Forgive my manners, Mr. Banks. Please, come in."

Sandy thanked her and stepped into the small home. The entry way led into a surprisingly spacious living room. Light spilled in from the front window and another on the side. Pictures adorned the walls, the fireplace mantle and every table in the room.

"Can I get you something to drink?" Gail asked.

"No thanks," Sandy said. "I'm fine."

"I was about to pour myself some coffee. There's plenty in the pot for two cups."

"Sure, then," Sandy said. "As long as it's no trouble."

"None at all." She motioned to the furniture in the living room. "Have a seat. I'll be right back."

Sandy glanced around. There was a short couch flanked by two easy chairs. He figured one belonged to her. The other had probably been Cal's. The idea of taking the old man's seat unsettled Sandy. It seemed like a matter of respect to him. He decided to sit on the couch instead.

Gail returned with two cups of coffee on a small tray a short time later. She set the tray down and looked up to see Sandy examining an eight-by-ten black and white photograph.

"That's Cal in his rookie year," she told him.

"He looks so young," Sandy said.

"Yes," Gail answered. "And so handsome. Here you are,

Mr. Banks."

She extended a cup to him.

Sandy took the cup and thanked her. He motioned toward the photograph. "You must have been proud."

Gail settled into her chair, cradling her own cup with both hands. "Oh, of course I was. Cal loved what he did. And he was good at it. I was terribly proud of him."

"You should be. He was a good man."

Gail hummed in agreement as she sipped her coffee. They sat in silence for a few moments before she spoke again. "I don't get visitors very often these days."

"No?"

She shook her head. "Oh, they came by frequently after Cal died. Quite a number of them, actually. But slowly, that changed. Fewer and fewer came by less and less often." She shrugged. "Now, I don't think any of the officers that worked closely with Cal are still on the force."

"Probably not many," Sandy agreed.

Gail let out another hum in agreement as she took another sip. She reached into her sweater pocket and removed a small silver flask. She held it up, proffering it to him.

Sandy raised an eyebrow. "What's that?"

"Just a little Bailey's," Gail said. She twisted the cap. "Cal and I always liked a little nip of it in our coffee."

Without a word, Sandy extended his cup toward her. Gail poured a generous dollop of Bailey's Irish Crème for him, then did the same for herself. Sandy waited until she'd twisted the cap back onto the flask and returned it to her sweater. Then he raised his cup.

"To Cal," he said.

She smiled and raised her own cup to touch his gently. "Always Cal," she whispered.

They drank, sipping the hot coffee. Sandy welcomed the warmth in the coffee and the liqueur. He sat quietly, enjoying the tranquil setting as the booze soothed his nerves. Gail sat nearby, sipping her coffee and saying nothing. For a while, Sandy felt as if he'd stepped outside of his life. Like maybe he'd found a tiny, temporary oasis in the middle of his crumbling world.

"Funny that I've never met you before, Mr. Banks," Gail finally said, breaking the silence.

Sandy shrugged. "Cal and I didn't socialize much outside of work, except for the occasional choir practice."

"I didn't think so," Gail said. "I would have remembered you. You didn't come by when he passed, either."

"No," Sandy said. "And I'm sorry for that."

Gail made another humming sound, though this time it was closer to a grunt and held a slightly reproving tone. She sipped her coffee.

"I went to see him," Sandy said. "Up at Holy Cross. After."

"Did you like the headstone?" she asked him.

Sandy shook his head. "I didn't see a headstone. Just the ground plaque."

Gail said nothing. She sipped her coffee.

Sandy smiled to himself. She's testing me, he thought. Smart old bird. He lifted his coffee and took a swallow.

She smiled slightly. "A little Bailey's is good in the afternoon. Don't you agree, Mr. Banks?"

"I do."

A few more quiet moments passed. Then Gail said, "He spoke of you."

"Cal?"

She nodded. "Yes. Near the end."

Sandy took another swallow of coffee and looked up at Gail. She wasn't looking at him, though. She stared at the picture of Cal Ridley. Her eyes held a faraway look.

"He kept asking me all kinds of questions," she said.

"About good and evil. I thought he was having a spiritual crisis. Like all those years of me prodding him to go to church were coming to a head. But I don't think that was it. Not anymore. Not exactly."

"What did he ask you?"

She smiled faintly. "About justice, mostly. If I thought the world was just. Which it isn't, of course. But he knew that." She turned her eyes to Sandy. "I imagine you know it, too, Mr. Banks."

"I do."

She nodded, then turned back to the photograph. "Cal was an idealist. He told me once that the world was in dire straits but that with enough good men, he could save it. Or at least the part of it that we lived in."

Sandy didn't reply.

"Near the end," Gail continued, "in those last few weeks, he seemed to have an urgency about him. As if something was bothering him, something he had to get off his chest."

Sandy tried not squirm in his seat. How much did Gail know?

"It was like he needed to know he was right," Gail said. "He wanted to be right with things, before he died."

"We all do," Sandy said softly.

Gail raised her eyebrows slightly at his words. "Do we? Yes, I suppose that's true. But Cal said he wanted to bring some justice into our corner of the world. So he came up with this idea of something he called the Four Horsemen. Did he talk about that with you?"

Silently, Sandy nodded.

Gail smiled. "I figured as much. He mentioned you when he talked about it. And Hank Gresham. Bill Blalock, too. And some younger man. Brian something?"

"Moore," Sandy whispered.

"That's it," Gail said. She nodded resolutely. "He said he

was going to get the four of you together. He would send you four the worst cases he came across where the bad men got away. And that you four would take care of those evil doers. You'd bring justice into their world."

"He said that?"

Gail nodded, glancing up at him with keen eyes. "And you say he talked to you about those things?"

Sandy nodded. "More than once. But it was just drunk talk. Drunk talk and wishes."

Gail didn't answer right away. He watched as she turned her head, staring at Cal's photo. Then she raised her coffee cup to her lips and sipped. Without looking at Sandy, she said, "Except he didn't talk about it like it was something he was going to do, Mr. Banks. He spoke about it more like something he'd already done. Something he wanted me to validate. Or to offer absolution."

Sandy didn't answer right away. He struggled with how to ask the question he'd come to ask, but couldn't think of a subtle way to do it.

Gail saved him the trouble. "He said it was his greatest act," she said quietly, "and his worst."

Sandy let a small smile touch his lips. "Was he sad that it was over?"

"Over?"

"Because he was…passing on?"

Gail shook his head. "I don't think so. He said he'd made arrangements. Secret arrangements. That, for better or worse, his little project would continue. He wouldn't say more than that, though. Perhaps you know something, Mr. Banks?"

Sandy resisted the urge to sigh in disappointment. He wasn't going to find a route to the Keeper here. He shrugged. "I don't know what was going on in his mind. I'm sorry."

Gail waved off his apology. "No need for apology. I eventually came to the same conclusion you did. He was frustrated, that's all. The Four Horsemen were merely a dying man's fantasy."

Sandy took another drink of his coffee to hide his relief.

"I told that same thing to the man who came to see me last week," Gail said.

Sandy stopped short, his mouth full of coffee. He felt his heart quicken. He swallowed quickly and asked her, "Someone came here last week to ask about Cal?"

Gail nodded. "Not just Cal, though. He asked about this Four Horsemen idea of Cal's, too."

"What did he ask?"

Gail didn't answer. She took a long drink of her coffee while looking at Cal's photo. Then she looked up at Sandy. "Isn't it strange, Mr. Banks? That he would come asking about some raving thoughts that my Cal had near the end of his life almost ten years ago? I thought it was. I thought perhaps Cal was foolish enough to have written down this idea somewhere. But if that were the case, why was someone coming to me now and not back when Cal passed?"

"I don't know."

Gail ignored his comment. "And then, just a week later, you show up on my doorstep." She shook her head. "That is an awful large coincidence, don't you think?"

Sandy's throat felt dry. His mind raced. When Gail looked over at him, he offered her no mask in his expression. He thought about telling her the truth, though he didn't know what good it would do, or how she would react.

Before he could speak further, she said, "But life is full of coincidences, isn't it? They happen by the bucket full, if you care to keep count. I think that's all it was."

Her smile was warm, her eyes knowing.

"Besides," she added, "I didn't like the man who came asking last week. He was polite but there was something about him I didn't trust. And Cal always told me to follow my instincts. He said that you don't have to know why you know something, you just have to know it."

Sandy chuckled lightly. "That sounds like Cal. Only, on the job, he would always add that knowing it isn't proving it."

It was Gail's turn to laugh. "That would be him. My big, tough lieutenant. He was hard on you all, wasn't he? On his men, I mean."

"At times," Sandy admitted. "But he was fair."

"Good," she said. "That's good."

"He was loyal, too."

She smiled. "Of course he was. And he believed in what he did. He was quite certain about that."

They sat in silence again. Sandy thought about Cal and the Four Horsemen. The Odoms file was a righteous file. Cal would have believed in it. Then he wondered about the unopened file under his car seat.

Sandy forced himself back on task. He considered the man who had visited Gail last week. If that man already knew about the concept of The Horsemen before he talked to Gail, and she shared those names with him…

"Mr. Banks?"

Sandy shook himself from his reverie. "Yes?"

"I get the feeling that you came here to ask me something."

He nodded. "I did, actually."

"I have to tell you, though," Gail said, "I really don't know any more about this than what I've already told you."

"I understand. Can I ask you one question, though?"

"Of course."

"Who was the man that came to talk to you? Was he FBI?"

Gail shook her head. "No, I don't think so. He didn't properly identify himself by his profession, actually."

"Did he use a name?"

"Yes. He said his name was Larson. George Larson. Do

you know that name?"

Sandy shook his head. "Was he alone? No partner?"

"Yes, he was alone."

"Did he wear a suit?"

She shook her head. "No, he was much more casually dressed. He wore a pair of those casual slacks…oh, what are they called?"

"Dockers?"

"Yes. And a short sleeved shirt. But one with a soft collar. And the little animal on the chest?"

"A polo shirt?"

"I think that's it, yes. But he wore very formal shoes," Gail added. "They were nicely shined. I remember that because it was the only thing I liked about him."

Sandy felt his stomach drop. "Formal shoes? What were they?"

Gail smiled. "He wore a pair of very stylish wingtips. They were quite stylish."

11

"That was dangerous," she said to him, stepping out of her heels. "He could have made you."

"Not a chance," he said. He slid off his belt, catching his holster as it came free. He put it on the motel room dresser. "He was a little suspicious, but when he saw me get into the BMW, that pretty much melted away."

"Where'd he go from there?"

He shook his head. "I don't know. I came here."

She sighed. "But did he – "

He stepped in close to her. His arm snaked around her waist and he pulled her close. "Relax. I got what we needed."

She cocked her head at him. "You're sure? He had it?"

"He has it. I watched him leave the post office with it. And I saw it on the front seat of his car when I did my walk past." He leaned in and kissed her neck. "Shouldn't be long now."

She wrapped her arms around his shoulders, her mind still whirring. "And you're still okay with all of this?"

He pulled his head away from her neck and stared her straight in the eye. "Okay with it? Babe, this is a gift from heaven. It is *the* answer."

"You're sure?" she asked, though she knew he was. They both were.

He smiled. "I'm positive."

She smiled back. He kissed her then, deep and passionate.

When they broke, he started to unbutton her blouse slowly. "I'll get into contact with my buddies at Fort Dix," he said. "They'll get me some background on this Banks character from when he was in the service."

"I don't know if we need that," she said, surprised that her voice was trembling slightly, but not because of the conversation.

"Intelligence is always worth it," he said, "especially when it comes cheap."

He finished with the last button and pulled the blouse back over her shoulders.

"You're ready for the next move?"

"Oh, I'm ready," he whispered, caressing her bare shoulder near her neck.

"We need to make sure," she said. Her words wavered in the face of anticipation. She lowered her own voice to match his. "He has to follow through."

"Don't worry," he murmured, lowering his mouth to her neck and kissing it softly. "I'll make sure he understands that. And I have a pretty good idea where he'll be heading next."

"Where?" she whispered.

"Shhhh. It won't be long now."

Not long, she thought. "You have a plan to motivate him?"

"I've got a good story, yeah." His hand drifted to the small of her back. "He'll believe what I tell him."

"And what about the other loose end?" She said. "There can't be anything that ties to us. Not if we're going to get out of here clean."

"I'll get to that, too," he said.

He worked his way slowly up her neck to the corner of her jaw. Then she turned her face. They found each other's lips, kissing again, and this time she gave herself completely.

12

Sandy drove without direction. He turned down residential streets and cruised slowly along, checking his rear-view mirror often. When he was finally satisfied that he wasn't being tailed, he considered his next move.

All the while, a single thought burned in his mind.

Who the hell was George Larson?

He didn't have an answer.

He drove for almost an hour, letting the mechanics of controlling the small Mazda become almost like a meditation. Neighborhoods he'd patrolled as a cop flitted by. He passed within blocks of several jobs he'd finished and resisted the urge to drive past them. That was all he needed, if the FBI was onto him. To be a suspect that returns to the scene of the crime like something out of a bad detective novel.

After an hour, he found himself driving north on Wall Street, the curiously residential arterial with a few small businesses sprinkled in every so often. As he crossed Francis, he realized where he was headed. Instead of resisting the inclination, he embraced it. Several blocks later, he made a right hand turn into Holy Cross cemetery.

It had been a long while since he'd visited the gravesite, but he drove to it unerringly. Once parked, he walked down the neat row of graves. Some were punctuated with large headstones, but Spokane was mostly a blue-collar town, so the majority were labeled with simple grave plaques.

He stopped, and looked down. A raised inscription rested on a darkened bronze background.

CALVIN JACOB RIDLEY.

And under that, the dates of his life span, followed by the epitaph.

BELOVED HUSBAND AND PUBLIC SERVANT.

"Don't forget 'Keeper of the Four Horsemen,'" Sandy whispered down at the stone. "What would you do now, you son of a bitch?"

He let memories of Cal on the job flow past his mind's eye like a ribbon of film. He remembered the grizzled lieutenant taking him aside when things were at their worst for Sandy. When it looked like IA was going to drill him and put him out of a job. How Ridley offered him another alternative. How he trusted Sandy. Even more than his own wife, apparently.

"At least until you got near the end," Sandy said aloud. "Then you started to run at the mouth a little, didn't you, Cal?"

The raised letters on the burial plaque stared up at him in silence.

Sandy stared back, thinking.

"What do I do now?" he finally asked aloud. "I can't get to the Keeper to warn him. Brian is probably already gone. Odoms the sick pervert is still walking above ground. Same thing for whoever is in the file in my car. All unfinished business."

He sighed. If the Feds were onto him, though…

"Maybe it's time to cut and run," he muttered. "It wouldn't be the first time in my life I had to do that."

Calvin Jacob Ridley's neatly lettered name spoke no words, but Sandy could imagine the man's presence. Cal always had an air about him that calmed men, settled them down. And he could break a complex situation down to its simplest terms. Sandy let that idea wash over him for a time. He listened to the wind in the trees that lined the cemetery as if the sound were Cal's words.

"It's done," he finally said. "I'm done."

A bittersweet relief welled up in his chest.

"It's time to move on," he said, looking down at Cal's grave marker. Then he smiled slightly. "Thanks, Cal."

Sandy turned to go.

One last thing to do, and then he would be a Horseman no more.

Brian Moore lived in a neighborhood filled with affordable rancher style homes. Sandy always thought of it as the kind of place that people stopped off when they left the realm of the rentals on their way to upper middle class suburbia. Of course, for some people, it was a permanent stop.

Most of the yards were small, but neatly tended. Some were enclosed with four foot chain link fences while others remained open. There were no driveways, so an array of cars lined the street. Sandy imagined every third home had children in it. This was still a neighborhood with some identity. People worked all week. Kids went to school. In the evenings and on the weekends, everyone played. Probably together.

He imagined coming home every night to a wife. Helping a son or daughter with homework while the wife made dinner. Sitting on the porch later, sipping a beer and talking to the neighbor about Gonzaga basketball.

Sandy pushed away the burst of sentimentality. There was no time to pine over a life not led. He'd made his choices.

Brian's house was dark blue with white trim. The paint was fading slightly, but had yet to begin to peel away from the wood siding.

Sandy passed the house, parking his car a half block away.

He sat for a short while, scanning the block for anything that raised his suspicions. All he could see was a quiet, working class neighborhood. It was exactly where you'd expect a cop to live, especially if he retired on a reduced pension.

When he was satisfied, he opened the car door and walked up the sidewalk. He noticed that Brian's lawn was starting to get long. The fact bothered him a little, but he couldn't figure out why. He didn't know how meticulous Brian was about such things. The fading paint spoke to at least a casual attitude toward home and yard maintenance. And maybe he'd simply been preoccupied with his decision to leave the Horsemen.

Sandy exhaled, letting the thought go. It didn't matter, anyway.

As he climbed the steps, he noticed that the angle of the door seemed slightly crooked. When he reached the top of the porch, he realized why. The door wasn't completely shut. A half-inch of the inner door jamb was exposed. It wasn't enough for a crack to appear, but it was clearly not closed.

Sandy paused, considering. Did Brian leave in a hurry and not shut the door all the way?

Or was something wrong?

Sandy wished for a moment that he had brought his gun with him. His mind flashed to one of Cal's sayings that he'd no doubt cadged from the National Rifle Association.

"Better to have a gun and not need it than to need a gun and not have it," the old lieutenant always chimed when the subject of carrying off duty came up.

Sandy didn't know if he *needed* a gun right then, but he sure as hell wished he had one.

It was probably nothing, he said to himself. People make the mistake of not closing the door securely all the time.

He frowned. People did, yeah. Not cops, ex or otherwise.

His finger snaked out toward the doorbell. He pressed the

button. Faintly, he could hear the two chime tones fill the interior of the house.

He stood and waited.

No answer.

After thirty seconds, he pressed the button again. This time he gave it two quick shots right on top of each other. The resulting chimes conveyed the same impatience he was feeling in his chest. Further down, in his stomach, a sense of unease had started to simmer.

Almost a minute passed with no answer.

Sandy stood, considering his options.

He could walk away. Maybe Brian was already gone. Maybe the unsecured door meant absolutely nothing. He'd tried to warn him, but maybe it wasn't even necessary. Maybe Brian was already in the wind.

Sandy took a deep breath and let it out slowly.

Maybe.

Or maybe he was inside. Maybe he was hurt. If he was, he might need help.

Or maybe, God forbid, he'd hurt himself. Maybe the guilt got to him. Maybe if Sandy went inside, he'd find Brian hanging in the shower stall, or sprawled out over the bed with a pistol next to him.

Sandy shook his head to clear the image. It faded from his mind, but not quickly.

Christ, he thought, if Brian needs my help, I have to go in. And if he had an attack of the guilts and did something stupid, who's to say he didn't leave some kind of confession lying around?

He had to go in. He had to know.

Sandy thought about walking around the house, looking through the windows. He rejected the idea. Brian's neighborhood didn't strike him as the nosy type, but it seemed like the kind of neighborhood where someone would notice a strange man walking around the neighbor's house checking windows. Those neighbors would almost certainly call the police.

So it was go inside or walk away. And he'd already decided he was going inside. Sandy turned his body, naturally blading his stance as he reached out and gave the door a firm shove.

The heavy wooden door swung inward, creaking slightly on its hinges. Sandy waited a moment, letting the smells of the house drift out to him. He braced himself for the possibility of that tell-tale odor of death.

Sandal wood incense greeted him instead.

Standing on the doorstep much longer was running the risk of attracting attention. Without further hesitation, Sandy stepped inside and closed the door behind him.

He sniffed again. The strongest odor remained incense, but the air seemed a little stale.

Sandy stood still and listened. From the kitchen, he heard the quiet hum of the refrigerator. Somewhere in the living room, a clock ticked lightly. Nothing else.

The interior of the house was lit up by the daylight that streamed in through the windows. None of the shades were drawn. Sandy saw nothing suspicious in the hallway.

So why was the hair on the back of his neck prickling?

He forced himself to step forward. Two steps and he was in the entry way to the living room. A modest loveseat and a coffee table were set up in front of a large screen television. A few magazines lay on the table next to the remote control. Other than that, nothing.

Sandy moved further down the hall. As he approached the door to the kitchen, the hallway took a sharp left. No doubt that led to the bedrooms. He'd have to check those.

But first, the kitchen.

Sandy stepped through the doorway.

Seated at the kitchen table to his right was the man from the Wal-Mart parking lot.

Adrenaline shot through Sandy, electrifying his limbs. He forced himself to remain still. His eyes automatically went first to the man's hands, looking for weapons. Seeing them empty, he returned to the man's face.

"Hello, Sandy," the man said. The scar on his lower lip stretched out as he smiled slightly. He pointed to the chair opposite him. "Why don't you sit down? We have a lot to talk about."

Sandy didn't move. "Who are you?" he asked.

The man's smile broadened. "I think you already know that."

Sandy nodded. "Yes, I do. You're George Larson."

The man's smile faltered slightly, but then returned even grander. "That is a name I use sometimes. But it's not who I really am."

Sandy wondered if the man had a gun. He wished he could see his waistline and his lap, but he couldn't from the angle he stood. He considered engaging but if the man was armed, then it wasn't likely Sandy could get around the table to him before he accessed a weapon. At least Sandy knew he could duck backwards through the doorway if the man made a move. "Then who are you?" he asked, stalling.

The man raised his eyebrows. "You haven't figured it out yet? That disappoints me."

"Sorry."

"Don't be. I imagine you've got a lot on your mind these days."

Sandy's eyes narrowed. "How would you know?"

The man chuckled. "I know a lot, Sandy. In fact, I know just about everything." He leaned forward. "You see, I'm the Keeper."

13

Sandy stood stock-still, staring at the man. His mind raced, trying to put together facts as quickly as possible.

Was this man telling the truth?

Was he the Keeper?

Was he a Fed? A local cop?

Larson motioned toward the chair again. "Please. Sit."

Sandy didn't move. "How do I know you're telling the truth?"

Larson pursed his lips and shrugged. "I guess you don't know for sure. But how else would I even know that title? The Keeper?"

"Maybe you're a cop."

"I am a cop. Just like you used to be."

Sandy shook his head. "No, not like that. I mean a fed. FBI or Justice, working some kind of rogue police case."

"I see your point," Larson conceded. "So what kind of proof do you want to show that I am who I say I am?"

Sandy remained standing. He considered all of the questions he could ask. Every single one incriminated him. And if this guy was planning to arrest him at the end of this conversation, he didn't want to add any ammunition to their case.

Larson smiled again. "Tough position to be in, huh? If I am a fed trying to bust you, pretty much anything you say jams you up."

Sandy listened for the crackle of distant police radios or the stamp of boots. He heard nothing.

"And if I am the Keeper, you have to be wondering why I am even here. So you're in a real tight spot right now, Mr. Sandy Banks." Larson leaned back in his chair. "So why don't you sit down and we'll solve a few mysteries, you and I."

Sandy shook his head. "I'll stand. You speak."

Larson shrugged. "All right. I can't blame you for being cautious. I'd let you frisk me for a wire, but I'm pretty sure you'd use the opportunity to take my gun from me. And until I'm sure that *you're* sure about who I am—" He shrugged and smiled coldly. "Well, that's just not a chance I'm willing to take."

"What are you doing here?" Sandy asked him.

"Looking for you."

"Why here?"

"Because I knew this is where'd you be."

Sandy wanted to ask him how he knew that, but he felt that the knowledge balance of power was already too skewed in Larson's favor. He didn't want to make that fact even clearer.

"What do you want?" he asked instead.

Larson regarded Sandy. His eyes seemed as friendly as they'd been in the Wal-Mart parking lot, but now Sandy could see an edge to his gaze. That cop edge. He should have spotted it before.

"It's simple," Larson said. "I want you to finish the job you started."

Sandy shook his head. "I don't know what you're talking about."

A patronizing smile crossed Larson's lips. "Okay. Don't admit to anything. That's smart. But you asked what I wanted, and that's what I want."

"I'm not going on any more fishing trips," Sandy said. "I'm done."

Larson chuckled. "Fishing trips? That's a clever little euphemism. I like it."

"I mean it," Sandy said. "Brian's done, and so am I."

Larson stopped chuckling. "Brian, huh? That's why you're quitting?"

"I'm not quitting anything. I'm just saying I can't help you with whatever you're talking about."

Larson sighed. "Jesus. This code-talking is getting old already."

Sandy didn't reply.

Larson stared at him for a long while. Finally, he said, "You have a job to finish, Sandy. You want to bail after that, well I guess you did your duty. But don't leave me hanging."

"It never ends," Sandy said, choosing his words carefully.

"I know," Larson said. "One shitbag replaces another. I realize that. But don't take off after all the time I spent researching these specific shitbags. If I'm going to have to see what they did every night in my dreams, at least let me know when I wake up that they're fucking dead."

Sandy looked at the man carefully. His suspicion and doubt wasn't as strong as it had been when Larson first called himself the Keeper. With every word the man said, more of it slipped away.

"They found Troy Collins, by the way," Larson said.

Sandy raised his eyebrows, but said nothing.

Larson smiled. "Mailman smelled something funny. Fire Department did a little B and E and found him in his living room. Homicide dicks are pretty sure it was a drug rip."

Sandy didn't reply.

"I don't know if that was you or Brian," Larson said, "but it was a good job, either way."

There was nothing for Sandy to say. He remained standing, silent.

Larson nodded as if Sandy had spoken. "I know, you aren't

going to talk about it. I might be a fed or be wired or whatever. But it's long past time I thanked you for your service, and told you that you've done well. Take the compliment in goddamn silence if you want to, but at least take it."

Sandy remained impassive. Finally, he said, "I don't know what you're talking about."

Larson laughed. "I figure that's about as close as I'll get to a 'you're welcome' from you," he said, "so I'll take it." He leaned forward. "But, Sandy, I need you to close out these last two files. Once you do that, you want to quit, go ahead."

Sandy shook his head. "No."

Larson sighed and leaned back. "Why not?"

Sandy didn't reply.

Larson chewed on his lip, considering. "All right, let's try this. Hypothetically, let's say a guy was being asked to finish a long term job. His boss wants him to do a couple more things before he retires. Why would a guy refuse to do that?"

Sandy bristled slightly at the word 'boss,' but he didn't respond.

"This is all just hypothetical," Larson said. "Not real." He waved his hand around in a circle. "Let's say we're talking about plumbers or something. A couple more leaks before the guy retires. Why not plug those leaks?"

Sandy considered. His mind ran through all of the possibilities. He reached back into his memories of criminal procedures and wondered if this was a safe avenue for him. His instincts were still singing out a danger song to him, but he couldn't pin down exactly why. Larson definitely knew a great deal about the Horsemen. He could be the Keeper. Sandy's mind was beginning to accept the possibility. But something was still not quite right.

"Hypothetically?" he finally asked.

Larson nodded. "Yeah. Story time."

Sandy considered his words before he spoke. "Maybe that

plumber is just tired of plugging leaks. Maybe it is just time to retire."

Larson nodded again. "Fair enough. What could that boss say or do to get the plumber to finish out the last two leaks before he retired, though?"

"Hypothetically?"

"Of course."

"Nothing," Sandy answered.

Larson looked disappointed.

Brian is gone, Sandy wanted to shout. They are all gone. I'm the last one and I don't want to do this anymore.

Instead, he stood in the kitchen without a word.

Larson sighed. "It's not like that plumber hasn't done his part," he said. "He has. But he can't just leave with the job unfinished."

"Why not?"

"He's like a soldier," Larson said. "He has a duty."

"A plumber with a duty?" Sandy asked.

Larson shrugged. "As long as we're weaving tales here, sure. Why not? He has a duty to finish the job."

"Maybe he's already finished," Sandy said.

"Well, hypothetically, maybe his boss tells him he needs to finish things *completely*."

"Hypothetically," Sandy said, "maybe he tells his *boss* to go fuck himself."

Larson's eyebrows shot up. Anger flashed momentarily in his eyes. For some reason, Sandy felt a sense of satisfaction in the display. The flash was gone almost as quickly as it had appeared, replaced by a look of resignation, tinged with sorrow.

"Don't make this difficult, Sandy," Larson said.

"I don't plan on making it anything at all," Sandy said. "Either I'm going to walk out of here or you're going to arrest me, but in either case, I don't know about any of the things you're talking about."

Larson sighed. "I wish there was a way to make this easier."

Sandy shook his head. "Nothing's easy."

"You're right," Larson agreed. "But see, here's the deal. I know Brian's not in the game anymore. I know he handed off his last file to you."

"You're making things up," Sandy said.

"No, I'm not. I know you've got the Odoms file. And I know you picked up the latest file. I followed you. From the little factory where Odoms works to post office to the Walmart parking lot. I saw you leave the building with the file. I saw it on your front seat in the parking lot."

"You sound like a fed with all that surveillance talk," Sandy said, but his mind raced. *So that's who's been following me all along.*

Larson shook his head. "No. I'm the man that Cal Ridley trusted with you guys. But now you're the last one. And I need you to finish the job."

Sandy almost winced at Cal's name. He considered asking Larson about his visit to Gail Ridley, but resisted the temptation. He'd probably already said too much if this guy was planning on arresting him in the next few minutes.

"I know a little about your history, you know," Larson said.

Sandy eyed him carefully, saying nothing.

"I pulled your personnel jacket down at headquarters," Larson went on. "I read all about your career with us."

Sandy set his jaw. "You may have read some facts in a file," he said. "But you don't anything about me."

Larson smiled slightly. "Oh, I don't agree. I know quite a bit about you. I know why you resigned from the police department. I know about that case. The one with the DV victim? I know that."

Sandy didn't reply. He gave Larson a hard look.

Larson seemed unfazed. "And it doesn't take a rocket scientist to figure out the reason you took Cal up on his offer to kill bad guys. I mean, if I left a battered woman alone in the house with some wife-beating piece of shit like you did, I'd probably want some redemption, too."

I didn't know he was there! Sandy raged inside.

The obvious answer echoed through his head.

You should have.

You failed her.

And she wasn't the first.

"So how many scumbags does it take to equal out to one innocent victim?" Larson asked.

"Fuck you," Sandy said, the tension in his voice electric and wavering with anger. "I'm leaving now, so arrest me if you're going to."

"I'm not going to arrest you," Larson said coldly. "But if you walk out that door without agreeing to finish the job, I will kill Brian Moore. That'd be one more victim you could add to your list of fuck ups."

Sandy felt his jaw drop slightly. With an effort, he clenched it shut.

Kill Brian?

Every thought of Larson being a fed or any kind of cop trying to set him up melted away. The realization had a calming effect on Sandy and spurred him to action.

Without hesitating, he burst forward, scrambling around the kitchen table toward Larson.

Larson showed no surprise. In one smooth motion, he brought up a handgun and leveled it at Sandy's chest.

Sandy stopped.

Larson smiled, but this time there was no warmth to the expression. "Sit the fuck down," he growled. He motioned to the far chair with the muzzle of his gun. "Right there."

Sandy obeyed, sliding the chair out from the table and settling into it.

Larson's cold smile disappeared. He set the Glock on the kitchen table in front of him. He met Sandy's eyes.

"There," he said. "Now we can talk."

14

Sandy stared at Larson for a long while, his mind whirring through possibilities. The black gun on the table in front of Larson sent his thoughts in entirely new directions.

Finally, he asked, "Where's Brian?"

Larson sighed. "You know, Sandy, if you'd just stayed a good soldier, things would have been just fine. You would have handled these last two files and then rode off into the sunset a hero or whatever. Why'd you have to make this difficult?"

"I asked you where Brian was."

Larson shrugged. "In a basement with a couple of my cousins, complaining about the quality of programming on basic cable."

"You *kidnapped* him?"

"Oh, don't get holier than thou on me now, Sandy," Larson said. "Not after what you've been doing for the past decade."

"What I did was different."

"Yeah, it is. You murdered those people."

Sandy clenched his jaw, his teeth grinding together. "They earned their fate," he gritted.

"Yes, they did," Larson agreed. "And as soon as you're done with your work, Brian will be released from the basement he's in, free to go wherever he pleases. You, too, for that matter."

"Why are you doing this?"

"I already told you why," Larson said. "I need you to finish the job. This seems to be the only way to make sure that happens."

Sandy shook his head. "I don't buy it."

"I don't give a fuck what you buy, as long as you finish – "

"No," Sandy interrupted. "This isn't about closure or some kind of emotional baggage for you. There's more to it than that."

Larson paused, a small smile playing on his lips. "Always the smart one, huh?" He scratched his cheek and watched Sandy. Then he said, "Put it this way. This isn't just about you and I any more. Sometimes outside interests get involved. And I made some promises that you—" he pointed at Sandy, "—are going to keep."

Sandy considered Larson's words. "You sold our services?"

"Why not? Plenty of wronged family members with cash out there, Sandy. We needed the money for the slush fund."

Sandy shook his head. "We're not mercenaries."

"Don't get so noble. You killed for money. By definition, that makes you a mercenary."

"No," Sandy said. "We killed for a cause."

"Well, then by definition that makes you a terrorist." Larson smiled. "Or a patriot, depending on which side eventually wins."

"I didn't sign on to make anyone rich," Sandy said.

"Rich?" Larson snorted. "It's not about getting rich. It's about keeping the project afloat. You think that it's easy to divert seizure money anymore?"

Sandy shrugged.

Larson shook his head. "Trust me, it's not. Fucking drug unit used to be a gold mine. Two for you, one for me, all that shit. Now they don't send the unit commander to DEA school. They send 'em to an accountant's school. That unit is tighter than a crab's ass now. Where else am I supposed to skim from? There's no money in busting burglars or dope fiends, just dealers. And forget white collar crime. You never even touch the actual money arresting those guys."

Larson leaned forward and met Sandy's eyes with his own. "So, you see, shutting down this whole operation is probably a good idea for everyone involved. It isn't sustainable any more. Hell, the world we live in, even the great silent majority out there wouldn't be in support of it. There's no stomach any-more for the dirty part of doing what needs done. It's time to put it to rest. But not until the entire job is finished."

"And if I don't finish it, you'll kill Brian?" Sandy asked, still not believing it.

Larson nodded. "It's a matter of survival."

"How's that?"

"If I don't carry through on this deal, the client goes to the press or the prosecutor's office," Larson explained. "Then all the cards come tumbling down."

"Don't tell me that. You should have insulated yourself better than that."

Larson shrugged. "Shoulda, coulda, woulda. It is what it is."

"You'd kill Brian to avoid prison?"

Larson raised his eyebrows in mild surprise. "You know what happens to cops in prison?"

Sandy shook his head in disbelief. "You're a traitor."

"Sticks and stones, Sandy. Sticks and stones." Larson gave him an expectant look. "Now, are we clear on where things stand?"

Reluctantly, Sandy nodded. "We're clear."

"Good," Larson said. "Now go do what you do best."

Sandy rose from his chair, turned and left without a word.

15

"*Victor-32?*" the radio squawked.

He glanced over at his partner, then back at the radio. "I think it's your turn," he said.

She shook her head. "I'm driving. You're the radio man."

"I answered up last time," he complained.

"Them's the rules," she told him.

He sighed and reached for the portable radio. "The rules suck," he said. "And so does your grammar." Then he depressed the transmit button and answered dutifully. "Victor-32, go ahead."

"*Any sign of him?*"

"None."

"*Did you change cars?*"

He looked at his partner, who rolled her eyes.

"You believe this asshole?" he asked her. He held the radio to his mouth but didn't push the transmit button. "Yes, you fucking derelict. We changed goddamn cars, just like you told us to. We're not idiots like you."

She smiled. "Like you have the balls to ever say that."

He smirked, depressed the button and snapped, "Affirmative."

"*Copy. I'm sending Victor-68 out to your twenty with the van. When he gets there, I want you to change over to the secondary site and assist Victor-44 at that location.*"

She groaned. "Babysitting a witness. That's worse than tailing."

He raised his eyebrows in agreement. "Copy," he transmitted, then dropped the radio on the seat between them. "You're answering that thing next time he calls," he told her.

"Not if I'm driving."

"Fine. Let's switch right now."

She shook her head. "I don't trust your driving."

"I'm a great driver."

"You drive like an epileptic with Tourette's."

He sighed. "Always with the exaggeration, you."

They were quiet for a few minutes. Then she said, "Maybe he'll show here at the house before we get bumped."

"Maybe monkeys will fly out of my ass and play a violin concerto."

She laughed a little. After a moment, her laughter became contagious and he chuckled at his own joke.

"Vivaldi, you figure?" she asked. "Or Mozart?"

"Hell," he said, "If they came out of my ass, I'd be surprised if they could scrape out *Mary Had a Little Lamb*."

"More like *Mary is on the Lam*," she suggested.

"Ba-duh-tssshhhh," he replied, miming hitting a drum snare and a cymbal.

They fell quiet again, watching the apartment. After a while, he looked over at her. "You know, this is kinda goofy."

"Goofy how?" she asked, not looking away from the target's apartment door.

"Instead of wasting all this time on this guy, we ought to be going after the crooks he smokes."

She turned to him then, her face registering a little surprise. "Really?"

He nodded, seemingly dead serious. "Why not? I'm sure if we put the same amount of federal resources into investigating those dirtbags, we'd find something to bust them on. It wouldn't be as good as shooting them, but it'd be a start."

"Give 'em three hots and a cot at the federal pen, huh?"

"Probably better than they deserve, but yeah."

"So now you're all in favor of murder, thinly veiled by righteous vigilantism?"

His eyes widened. "Wow. Someone went and got a Master's Degree in Big Fucking Words."

"No big words in there, chopstick." She smiled. "It's all in how you put them together."

"You want to talk putting things together?" He jerked his thumb in the direction of the target apartment. "If our intel is solid and this guy has really been knocking off scumbags for *twelve* years, *that's* together."

"He's a vigilante, not a hero."

"You think so? Bernard Goetz was a vigilante and a lot of people figured him for a hero."

She sighed. "*If* you believe Goetz's own account of events, he acted in self-defense. Our guy is basically an assassin. Big difference."

He sighed. "World is probably a better place without the guys he's iced."

"Probably. But who gave him the okay to make that decision? That's why we have courts and laws and judges."

"Judges who routinely let dirtballs off on technicalities."

"The law is for everyone," she said. "If you only let it apply to the people you like, you end up with –"

"Justice?"

She smiled. "No. Despotism."

"Huh?"

"Fascism?"

"Huh?"

"Oh, come on. You know that one."

He squinted. "I fail to see what fashion has to do with our current discussion."

"Now you're being deliberately obtuse."

"Stop talking like a college graduate," he said.

"I *am* a college graduate. So are you."

He grinned. "Yeah. Tim Stanley's College of Culinary Arts. Good thing the Bureau doesn't check transcripts very closely, or I'd still be working security gigs."

She shook her head. "You're a dork. How does your wife put up with you?"

"She is routinely overcome with lust due to my good looks, I suppose."

"This is Chelsea, or did you divorce her and marry a blind woman?"

"Ha. Ha. Ha." He sat quietly for a moment, then started humming *Mary Had a Little Lamb* lightly.

She recognized the tune after a couple of measures.

"Not funny anymore," she told him. "Don't go to the well too many times for one joke."

"Hey," he said, "something works for me, I stick with it."

"Probably why you try new things constantly."

"I'd like to try having a day off and getting some sleep. That'd be something new."

"Soon enough," she said. "Even our glory hound SAC isn't going to let this go on forever."

He took a deep breath and let it out. "Yeah, I suppose." He thought about it for a moment, then added, "Unless *that's* where the promotion is in it for him."

"Of course."

"Asshole," he muttered.

"Asshole," she agreed.

16

Sandy drove less than a mile from Brian's house, when he pulled up to the curb at a small city park. He sat in the car for a moment, then got out and strolled across the grass to a wooden picnic bench.

The park was sparsely populated. A trio of boys shot baskets on the other side on a concrete basketball court. Every time the ball went in the basket, it rattled the chain netting. A middle-aged woman walked a basset hound around the edge of the park. Sandy watched them without seeing any of them, his mind tackling his situation.

He should just slip away. That was the safest bet. Let the cards come tumbling down, as Larson put it, but only after he was gone. If Larson was going to go rogue like this, screw him.

But that screwed Brian. Sandy didn't know if Larson would actually kill Brian, but he wasn't willing to risk it. Besides, even if he was lying about that part, Larson would take Brian down with him. Sandy had no doubt of that. So he couldn't desert Brian. He'd been one of the Horsemen. Sandy had a duty.

He swallowed thickly, considering the task before him.

He had to finish with Odoms.

Then he had to finish this new file, which he hadn't even opened yet.

Not get caught.

And make sure Brian was actually released.

"Easy as pie," Sandy muttered sarcastically.

He sat and watched the kids play round ball for another twenty minutes. Then he rose from the picnic table. Might as well go home, he figured. Now that he knew who'd been tailing him, the heat was off.

That night, he lay in his bed staring at the ceiling. Something was nagging at him, but he couldn't quite pin it down. He ran through his conversation with Larson over and over again. He chastised himself for the questions he should have asked but didn't.

Eventually, he turned his mind to Odoms. That would have to be first. And the sooner the better. Tomorrow. Maybe finish both, if he could make it work. He didn't like abandoning the methodical approach he'd used all these years, but what choice did he have? Every moment he waited to finish the job was another moment Brian was in captivity. He might be watching bad cable TV like Larson said, but Sandy wasn't betting things were quite that easy.

He glanced at the green digital numbers on his clock. 10:14, they read.

Sandy reached out and set the alarm for 4:00 AM. Then he lay in bed, staring at the ceiling. He saw Brian sitting in a chair. Duct tape held him in place at his wrists and ankles.

He pushed the image away. It was replaced with images of Yvonne Lewis flashing through his mind. Her bruised cheek. The trickle of blood at the corner of her mouth. The way she held her forearm but refused to acknowledge it was injured.

Him in his dark blue wool uniform, a badge on his chest.

"When did he leave?" he'd asked her.

"Just a minute before you got here." Tears streamed down her cheeks. "Maybe less. I don't know."

"Any idea where he'd go?"

She shook her head. "Some bar, maybe."

"You're sure you're okay?"

A frightened nod. "I'll be fine. I'll go to my sister's house after you leave."

And so he took the report. He asked her all the questions. He took photographs of her face. He knew that when he wrote it all up, there'd be a warrant for her wife-beater of a husband. Which was fine with him. As far as he was concerned, there was a special corner in hell for those bastards.

He left, and an hour later the cops were back at that small house. Only this time, she wasn't talking. And the place was full of homicide detectives and a shift commander screaming at him.

He was hiding in the house the whole time, you dumb son of a bitch!

Sandy winced at the memory, even all these years later. With a conscious effort, he took a deep breath, let it out and tried to push those thoughts away.

When he was finally successful, though, older demons came to haunt him.

17

*Y*ou're dreaming, Sandy.

"I know," he tried to say, but he couldn't make his mouth work.

You're a child.

"I don't want to be," he tried to say, but the words stuck in his throat.

Hazy images floated before his eyes. Music played. Distant, and muffled. Was it the ice cream truck? He felt sure it was summer. The coming of the ice cream truck was more important to a kid than the messiah, though he knew well enough not to say so. He didn't have a father to put a whipping on him for saying something like that, but one razor sharp look from Pastor Terence was just as bad. Besides, his mother would pick up on the good father's disapproval. Just because she didn't believe so much in the strap didn't mean she wouldn't bring it out and dust it off for a special occasion, such as saying something the good pastor disapproved of.

Why was he thinking about the priest? He hadn't been a bad guy, really. Much better than the one who eventually came to live under Sandy's own roof. Pastor Terence had never made him nervous in any way other than that particular unease that any adult in authority might cause. So far as he knew, the man had been a true servant of the cloth.

So why think of him with ice cream music playing?

Sandy squinted through the haze. Images of polished wood came into focus. The music grew louder and more clear.

Not ice cream music, he realized.

Organ music.

From the church. And now he recognized the song. It had been years since he'd heard it. Maybe since that day.

Today.

You're dreaming.

"I know," he tried to say, but couldn't form words. He was able to summon a whimper. *No more.*

The song was about being lifted up on eagle's wings. During the years that he valued the ice cream truck over the second coming of the Messiah, it was his favorite church song. He imagined a giant eagle swooping down, landing with a powerful blast of air from its wings. He'd climb aboard and the great bird would spring into the sky once more. Wind would flow through his hair and he could see for miles and miles and miles…

But as the wood hues became crystal clear, he saw that he was in his mother's church. Bright sunlight shone through the stained glass. The song filled every corner of the worship area, and suddenly, he hated it.

Everything was so big. Men were giants. Pastor Terence's voice boomed, filling the air with his off-key singing.

He looked up to his right. His mother sat there, her face streaked with tears. She glanced down at him and he saw the loss in her eyes. Saw it with a child's knowledge, separate from his adult understanding.

She forced a momentary smile, but it wilted right away. Instead, she squeezed his hand.

He looked ahead. The long, huge coffin of dark wood stood in stark contrast to the lighter hues of the wood that the church was made of.

You know who's in that coffin, don't you?

"Yes," he whispered, and this time his words found voice.

And then the color faded. The light left the room. The pews and the walls seemed to be imbued with a darker, more malevolent wood. It was a smaller place, but it was the same place, and he was still dreaming.

The casket was smaller, too, and it had a reddish tint to the shined exterior. Almost a feminine quality.

There was no one to his right this time.

He looked to his left.

Janet, her head bowed. Sobbing quietly.

He reached out to touch her shoulder.

And was pulled backward to the ground.

He hit the ground hard, much too hard for a dream. This had to be real. But he couldn't see anything in the dark. Could only smell beer and cigarettes. He scrambled to his feet, instinctively raising his hands to defend himself.

"You little no-account bastard!" he screamed at Sandy.

In the near blackness, his dim form to shape. Huge head. Jug ears. Massive forearms and hands like hammers. But a soft gut. Always a soft gut.

"That's the last time you'll stick your nose in my business!" he shouted at Sandy, jabbing his finger for emphasis.

He knew the reply –

It's my mother! That's my business!

–but didn't voice it now. Instead he felt along his belt.

Nothing.

"It's my wife, goddammit!" he roared at Sandy. It didn't seem to matter that Sandy hadn't answered him. He was dreaming and things worked different in dreams.

He didn't answer again, even though he knew the words by heart.

You've got no right to hit my mother!

His hands patted his pockets.

There. In the back pocket.

"I'll do whatever I goddamn well please! I'm the man of this house!"

No, you're not. You'll never be the man of this house. You'll never measure up to him.

And he'd said the one thing that was unforgiveable.

"You little son of a bitch," he growled. "I'll show you what a big man can do."

The shadow shifted as he surged forward. Sandy wrapped his hand around the handle in his back pocket and pulled it free. In the darkness, he flicked his wrist in a practiced motion. The blade snapped open with a cold click.

He seemed to falter for a second, but Sandy didn't wait. He stepped forward and drove the knife into that soft gut. Drove it hard and sure and straight and with all his strength.

And then…that same goddamn song, forever ruined by three deaths. He never wanted to hear it again. Not in the waking world, and not here. But he couldn't pull free of the notes, or the grip that the polished wood and stained glass windows seemed to hold.

They conspired together and held him there until dawn.

18

"**H**e was there, then?"

Larson smiled. "Of course he was. This guy is as predictable as sunshine in the desert, baby."

"Tell me again what he said."

Larson sighed. "He didn't say much. He did try to play the noble card a little bit. Once I told him that it was either finish the job or I'd kill Brian Moore, he went along with the program."

"That was a dangerous play. What if Brian Moore suddenly shows up again?"

Larson shook his head. "He's in the wind. Why would he come back?"

"He's got a house to sell. That's a lot of money to walk away from."

"If he's smart, he can do that through a local lawyer while he's in the Cayman Islands or someplace like that," Larson said.

"That's where we should go. Or some place without extradition, just in case."

He smiled. "We're going to get out of here clean. There's no reason to worry about extradition."

"Anywhere we go, we'll need money. There's barely enough for a plane ticket left in the slush fund Ridley set up."

Larson scoffed. "These guys should've stopped being paid

a long time ago. That slush fund was probably pretty flush at one time." He shook his head ruefully, then shrugged. "We'll get all the money we need once Sandy finishes the job, though."

She frowned. "I wish there was another way."

"Hey," Larson said, "you want to live comfortably or you want to scramble around for dollars? Neither one of us has enough retirement yet to keep us above the poverty line. I don't know about you, but I don't want to stay here another twelve years so I can pay half my retirement to an ex-wife."

"I only have seven years left until I'm fully vested," she said. "We could get by on what I'd make."

"We could *scrape by* on what you'll get." He shook his head. "Meanwhile, this golden opportunity is gone. It won't come again. The slush fund is dried up. The last of the Horsemen is moving on. I'm about to lose the house and every other goddamn thing, Linda. Jesus, you want to choose *now* to get cold feet?"

She moved closer to him, put her arms around his chest. "No, no. I'm sorry. You're right."

"Fuckin' A, I'm right." He reached out and caressed her cheek. "Just a little longer, baby. Inside of three months, we'll be laughing about this on a beach over margaritas. I promise."

"I believe you," she whispered.

They were quiet for a few moments. Then she sighed. "I wish Brian hadn't chosen now to disappear. It complicates matters."

Larson shrugged. "What do we care? Banks will take care of business. We'll get done what we want done. Then he'll disappear. Life will go on."

"You make it sound so easy."

"It is easy."

"If it's so easy, why haven't you taken care of the other loose end yet?"

Larson scowled. "I will. Right after I leave here."

"Just asking," she said, her voice growing harder. "We can't have anything pointing back at you. If it points back at you, it will eventually point back to me."

"I know."

"And we can't have that."

"I said I know," he snapped.

"Just making sure we're clear," she said. She remained silent for a few moments, then asked him, "What if Banks wants proof that Brian's alive? That we released him?"

Larson shook his head. "I'll tell him I cut Brian loose and told him to contact him on his own. It's not my fault if he chooses not to."

"And if Banks doesn't believe you?"

"Fuck I care what he believes? He gets antsy, I'll tell him there's a file that has all the information in it about the Four Horsemen. It's with my make-believe cousin. If anything remotely suspicious happens to me, it goes to the U.S. Attorney's office. That'd bring the entire weight of the federal government down on his shoulders." Larson shook his head again. "He'll back off when he hears that."

"Too bad it's bullshit," she said.

"Bullshit rules the world, honey," he told her.

19

Sandy jogged toward Odoms's house dressed in his long sweats and a gray hooded sweatshirt. He trotted along slowly, keeping his head focused straight ahead, using his peripheral vision to scope out the scene.

The house was still dark. Odoms wouldn't be up for another hour, if he kept to his usual schedule.

Sandy spotted a surveillance car a half block up from the target house. Two men sat inside, though one looked to be reclined in the passenger seat, sleeping. The partially fogged window and the rumpled look of both men told Sandy they'd probably been there all night.

Sandy's mind raced. Were these the Keeper's men, there to make sure he did the job?

Or was it a trap?

If it were a trap, why would the Keeper want to set him up?

Sandy jogged past the house and down the block. There were too many possibilities for things to go wrong here. He didn't like the idea of cops parked up the street from a target while he was inside, even if they did answer to Larson.

He returned to his car. He started the engine and let it idle while he thought. After a few minutes, he decided Odoms could wait, at least until there wasn't an audience. He didn't know what Larson's endgame was, but he'd feel better about it if there weren't any witnesses to anything he did.

Sandy reached under his seat where he'd tucked away his .45 and the suppressor. Underneath them was the other file. He pulled it out, tore open the edge of the envelope, and looked inside for the first time.

This one was thin. He glanced at the label.

Kelly Caper, it read. And underneath that, Murder x 2/J.

"So he's a kid killer," Sandy murmured. That was good. It made things easier on him.

Sandy flipped open the file. A photograph of a smiling blonde woman in her late forties stared up at him.

He scowled. A woman? He'd never had a file come through with a woman before. Hank had one once, but that was the only one he could remember ever coming through.

Sandy skipped the biographical data and went straight to the summary. He skimmed through the report and immediately saw why Larson had selected this one. Kelly Caper had drowned both of her children in the bathtub rather than lose custody of them to her own mother.

He bit his lip. Those were the actions of an insane person. He wasn't as comfortable with insanity in this context. It wasn't exactly like killing an innocent, but it wasn't the same as executing evil, either.

Sandy took a deep breath and let it out. "Fuck it," he said. Anyone who does the heinous things he'd seen as a cop or in the files since becoming a Horseman had to be some kind of insane, anyway, right? Karma didn't always have to revolve around intent.

He glanced back up at the biographical data. He read the address. Then he dropped the car into gear and pulled away from the curb.

It was time for a cold call.

When he reached her street, Sandy scanned the area for any

surveillance vehicles. There were no cars parked on the streets or in the driveways. He wondered if Larson had surveillance set up in one of the neighboring houses. He peered into the windows as he rolled past, but saw nothing suspicious.

Her neighborhood was solidly upper middle class. Every garage was designed to hold at least three cars. The lawns were huge and almost certainly professionally maintained. Sandy imagined that practically every one of these houses was alarmed.

He cruised by the target residence, a dark red brick two-story that was at the bottom end of the price range for this part of town. The street was still empty and quiet. Sandy figured that this crowd, those that worked anyway, probably enjoyed routine 9-to-5 banker's hours.

Any car, especially one as proletariat as Sandy's, would stand out parked on the street in this neighborhood. So he drove around, looking for someplace non-descript to stop. A block away and on the next street over, he found a home for sale. He pulled into the driveway and parked.

From under the seat, he retrieved his .45. He screwed the suppressor onto the muzzle while staring at the woman's photograph, burning her features into his mind. Then he slid his hand holding the gun into the pouch pocket in his sweatshirt, got out of the car and flipped up the hood of his sweatshirt. He started jogging slowly in the direction of the target's house.

No cars passed him on the light trot over. As he approached the house, he slowed to a walk, pretending to be cooling off from a run. Without pause, he walked up the driveway. He'd spied a gate in the six foot fence that butted up to the house. The walkway branched off, providing a path to the front door and to the gate. Sandy went to the gate.

Hoping that it wasn't locked, he pulled the latch. The gate opened easily on oiled hinges. He paused a moment, wondering if there might be a dog in the back yard. Dogs were worse for him than burglar alarms.

Sandy heard no growling or barking nor any footsteps.

Good. No dog. Probably still an alarm to deal with, though.

He stepped into the back yard. The concrete path disappeared, replaced by heart-shaped stepping stones. Each one had a child's handprints, along with an age and a name.

Alicia, age five. A clumsy happy face was drawn underneath.

Tanner, age three. Tiny fingers.

Alicia, age seven.

Tanner, age four.

Alicia, age nine. This one was encrusted with marbles made to look like jewels. Sandy imagined a beautiful child dreaming of fairies, unicorns and being a princess.

His jaw set as he continued up the path. He diverted his eyes from the stones to the house to his left. A single window above the garage was the only potential threat. The window was dark.

He looked at the side of the target house. His eyes came to rest on a gray box with wires coming out of it. Even at a distance, he could identify the various uses; the thick black coaxial for the cable television, the thinner gray for the telephone and a round white cable that he guessed powered the security system.

Sandy withdrew his Leatherman multi-tool and flipped it open to the wire cutter. He let the .45 hang in its pouch, took hold of the telephone wire and snipped it. Then he grabbed onto the white cable and nestled it into the crook of the wire cutters.

He paused. Some systems were wired with an alternative power source. This allowed the alarm to trigger if the main source of power were disrupted. If he clipped the cable, he ran the risk of setting off the alarm in a neighborhood that he was pretty sure would bring all sorts of witnesses out of the fancy woodwork.

Still, the alternative power source was an expensive feature. Sandy guessed that whoever owned this place was stretching a little bit to get into the neighborhood. Everyone else had an alarm system, so they'd have to get one, too. But they didn't necessarily need the Cadillac model.

Sandy stared down at the white cable. The very fact that it was exposed and not in a secure box only reinforced his theory. This was a bargain level security set-up.

But if it wasn't…

Sandy clenched his jaw.

Sometimes, he thought, *you just have to forge ahead.*

He snipped the cable.

Nothing happened.

Quickly, he slipped the Leatherman tool back onto the belt he wore under his sweats. He gripped the handle of the .45 and continued along the stepping stones, not looking down.

As he reached the corner and looked into the backyard, he was confronted with a wide deck patio with heavy plastic chairs and a round table in the center. He paused, his eyes scanning the neighbors' homes above the fence line. He was much more exposed here. Now he had three different houses to worry about. Anyone on the second floor looking out a window would be able to see him easily. He would have to act quickly.

Hopefully, they're all still asleep, he thought, *because I'm committed now.*

Sandy rounded the corner. A large glass sliding door led from the house onto the patio. On the other side of the slider was a spacious kitchen. A blonde woman stood near the sink, pouring coffee.

Sandy did a double take. In the reflection of the stainless

steel stove backing, he saw familiar features. It was her. Kelly Caper.

His reaction was automatic. Without thinking, he leveled the .45 at the woman and fired through the slider.

The first shot clacked as the slide mechanism cycled. The bullet blasted through the glass, leaving a large, fist-sized hole. Thick cracks immediately radiated outward.

The woman staggered against the counter. The coffee pot fell from her hand and shattered on the floor. Oddly, the cup remained clutched in her left hand. Coffee sloshed out of it and splashed onto the counter.

Sandy's second shot went through the weakened glass two inches from the first hole. Behind her, wood splintered away from where the bullet struck the cabinet.

The cracks in the slider door deepened and lengthened. Huge chunks of glass broke away and crashed to the floor.

The woman didn't react to the second shot. She turned toward Sandy, a stunned look on her face.

Sandy strode purposefully through the large hole in the slider. He kept the gun leveled at her as he shouldered aside a dangling chunk of glass. It crashed to the ground behind him.

Her confused gaze settled upon his face. Her lips formed a question.

"Whuh—"she uttered.

Sandy cut her off with two quick rounds. The first caught her in the left breast, a perfect heart shot. The second one was a head shot, opening a dark hole above her left eye. A spray of blood, bone and brain matter splattered against the light oak cupboards behind her.

She toppled to the ground.

Sandy moved around the large center counter, his gun trained on his target. When he got a look at her, he lowered the gun. She lay still, gazing upward, a confused expression frozen on her face. She still clutched the handle of the now broken coffee cup in her left hand.

Without hesitation, Sandy backed away. He went around the island counter and to the long hallway that he figured led to the front door. He had to get out of the house before any prying eyes came out of any of the neighbors' houses.

His mind recited his exit strategy automatically. Out the front door, start jogging in the opposite direction of his car, then cut across to the car as quickly as possible. Drive one direction at the speed limit until he was out of the area.

He walked down a hallway lined with pictures, pulling his sweatshirt hood forward.

Simple plan. Not always easy to pull off.

He stopped suddenly, his peripheral vision catching sight of something. He took a step backward, turned and looked closer, unsure of his own eyes. He pulled the hood back slowly as he stared at large photograph on the wall. His stomach sank.

"Je – *sus*," he whispered.

She was in the picture. Kelly Caper. She looked easily ten years younger. Flanked by two teenagers.

"Alicia," Sandy said, shaking his head. "Tanner."

Not dead.

Not drowned.

He stared at the photograph. Next to a smiling version of the dead woman in the kitchen and surrounded by two beaming teenage children, George Larson grinned out at him.

"You son of a bitch," Sandy growled at the picture. "You set me up."

And you fell for it.

Sandy smashed the butt end of his .45 into the face of Larson's photo. The shattering glass reminded him of the slider door from moments ago.

"Mother*fucker!*" Sandy shouted. Rage bubbled up in his

chest and shot out to his arms and legs. He smashed the picture a second time, wishing it was Larson's face. He wanted to scream. He wanted to rip Larson limb from limb.

He took a deep, shuddering breath, trying to bring his rage under control. He turned and walked back into the kitchen. He stopped in the doorway, staring down at the still body of the woman he'd just murdered.

"Jesus," he muttered again.

Her confused stare, an accusation. The first tendrils of black guilt crept into the roiling anger that burned in Sandy's stomach. He stood above her, wondering if her name was even Kelly. Why she was dead. What had she done that was so terrible that Larson wanted her killed?

He heard the creak of footsteps on the wood patio a moment before the voice rang out.

"FBI! Don't you move!"

20

Sandy fired in the direction of the voice without thinking. By the time his eyes caught up with his own reaction, he saw a chubby man in suit cry out in pain and clutch at his thigh. The man crashed to the ground, howling in pain.

The woman in a pants suit behind him held her gun pointed to the ground in classic police fashion. She glanced involuntarily down at her partner as he fell, surprise and horror plain on her face. In that moment, Sandy shifted his aim to her.

"Drop it," he told her forcefully. "Or I'll blow a hole in your chest big enough to walk through."

She turned back to Sandy. Her eyes widened at the sight of the .45 trained on her. Her hand twitched.

Sandy leaned forward slightly. "Don't," he growled. "You are *not* fast enough."

She paused, then looked back down at her partner. He held his thigh, moaning in pain and rocking back and forth. His gun lay near his feet. His pants were already soaked through with blood.

"Put the gun down," Sandy ordered her, "and I'll let you help him."

The woman looked back at him, studying his face as if she were trying to gauge how trustworthy he might be.

"From the amount of blood I'm seeing, I'm guessing that's

an artery I hit," Sandy said. "You don't have much time."

"Neither do you," she replied, her voice shaking slightly but surprisingly strong. "Police are on the way."

Sandy shrugged, even though he felt a tinge of panic nibbling at the edge of his composure. "So he dies and I have you as a hostage. Or you drop your gun, he survives and I have two hostages."

She studied him a moment longer, then crouched down and put her gun on the kitchen floor.

"Slide it over," Sandy ordered her.

She slid the pistol across the floor toward him. It stopped two feet away.

"Now his," Sandy said, gesturing at the identical pistol next to the man's feet.

She reached over the wounded man and shoved the gun in Sandy's direction.

"His I.D.," Sandy said.

"He's bleeding to death!" she shouted.

"Then you better hurry," Sandy said, not raising his voice.

Angrily, she fished a billfold out of the man's inside jacket pocket and tossed it toward Sandy. It landed with a slapping sound at his feet.

"Direct pressure," he told her. "And hard. Harder than you think."

She turned her attention to her wounded partner. She found the wound and pushed down hard, leaning downward. The man cried out in pain again.

"Oh fuck," he yelled. "That hurts!"

Sandy kept his eyes on the pair as he crouched down to pick up the billfold. He flipped it open. An FBI badge and credentials stared out at him.

"Special Agent Scott McNichol," he said aloud. He looked up at her. "And you?"

"Go to hell," she replied, her voice still wavering. This

time, though, Sandy thought it was more due to anger.

Sandy dropped the billfold to the ground and stood up. He took two steps toward the agents, then stopped and dropped into a catcher's crouch. "What are you doing here?" he asked them.

"What are *you* doing *here*?" she snapped back.

Here?

"What's that supposed to mean?"

She ignored him. "Hang in there, Scott," she told her partner in hushed tones. "It's going to be fine. Help is coming. You're going to be all right."

Agent McNichol closed his eyes and groaned.

Sandy pointed the .45 directly at her. "Listen," he growled through clenched teeth. "I shoot you, he bleeds out. Is that how you want it?"

She shot him a murderous glare. "You cold-hearted bastard," she spat out at him.

"I don't have time for this," Sandy snapped.

"You're goddamn right you don't," she snapped right back at him. "Cops are on their way. You're fucked."

Sandy rose, took another step toward her and pressed the gun against her forehead. "Maybe we're all fucked," he whispered intensely. "Or maybe I get my answers and then I get out of here. Agent McNichol lives. So do you."

"Maybe you go to hell," she said, not looking at him.

Sandy moved the gun away from her head and fired a round into the floor near her knee. "Maybe," he said. "Maybe we all go there together. Your call."

She started to shake her head at him, but McNichol interrupted her with a moan. "Jesus, Lori. Just tell him," he said through gritted teeth. "I'm dying."

Sandy met her gaze. She sighed and nodded.

"What are you doing here?" he asked her.

"Following you," she replied.

"Why?"

"In case you made a move."

"How did you know about this target?"

"About this target?" She shook her head. "We didn't. We were following you. When we heard the glass break, we figured out what you were doing."

Sandy considered her words. In the distance, he heard the muted yelp and wail of a police siren. Graveyard officers had been rousted from their paperwork and early morning coffee and were on the way.

"You're running out of time," Agent Lori told him without looking up from her bloody hands. She continued to press downward.

"Odoms," Sandy said, realizing. "You were onto Odoms."

"You're a fucking genius," she said.

Sandy shook his head. "The surveillance outside his house is FBI."

She nodded.

"And Odoms? Inside?"

"No." She shook her head. "Another agent. Odoms has been relocated."

Murdering Scumbag Protection Program, Sandy thought. Then another question occurred to him. "The file?"

"Doctored," she said. "It has correct information, but all the photos were doctored to put our agent's image in his place."

"Another set up," Sandy muttered.

"Another?" she asked. Her gaze went from McNichol's wound to meet Sandy's eyes. "What does that mean?"

A second set of sirens joined the first, then a third. The sounds grew closer and louder.

Sandy waved off her question with the muzzle of his .45. "How did you know about the Odoms file?" he asked. "How did you even know about this operation?"

Agent Lori paused. Sandy moved the muzzle off of her and onto McNichol. "I have about ten seconds before I hit the point of no return," he told her.

She shuddered slightly. Then she whispered, "Brian Moore."

Sandy's eyes narrowed. "You were onto Brian?"

"No," the agent said. Her eyes flicked to the .45 leveled at McNichol. "He's our C.I."

"What?" Sandy shook his head in disbelief.

"Brian Moore is working for us. He's our snitch."

Sandy shook his head again, her words not registering. *"Brian?"*

She nodded without looking at him.

"Since when?"

The agent swallowed. Her eyes flicked down to her partner then back to Sandy. "Maybe a month or so."

"Christ," Sandy muttered, his stomach sinking. "He was wired when he came to my apartment the other day, wasn't he?"

She gave him a short nod.

"Christ," he repeated. He wanted to ask more questions, but the yelp and wail of the police sirens were getting too close. He was out of time. If he didn't leave now, it was all over. He rose to his feet.

"Has his bleeding slowed down?" Sandy asked her.

"What do you care?" she snapped back.

Without a word, Sandy turned and ran down the hallway to the front door.

21

Sandy slammed the door behind him and set off at a trot, heading in the direction of his car. Then he realized that hiding in plain sight wouldn't work. Even with her bloody hands pressing on McNichol's thigh, he was pretty sure Agent Lori What's-her-name would find a way to broadcast his description to the responding local police.

He broke into a steady run, loping down the street. His car was about three blocks away. He could cover that in less than a minute. But he'd cut it close with the responding police units, staying as long as he could in the kitchen with the interrogation. There was no way he was going to make it to his car before police arrived in the area. He could only hope that they approached from a different direction than the one he was heading in. Most cops would have the Pavlovian response of heading directly to the house. The smart ones would anticipate his moves and try to cut him off.

Sandy hoped for cops who were rummy from working all night, running on automatic pilot. He doubted he'd get his wish. Sirens were blaring all over the neighborhood now. In moments, residents would start poking their heads out to see what the big production was. Some would have the sense to call 911 about a man running full tilt in a gray sweat suit.

Ahead, he needed to make a right. Two more blocks down that street, around the corner to the left and two houses up sat his Mazda.

As he pumped his legs, he forced his mind to stay clear the revelations of a few moments ago. He tucked away the rage for Larson and the swirling, ambivalent feeling about Brian's betrayal. He could examine that when he had time to think. Right now—

A police car screamed around the corner ahead of him. A patrol officer looked at Sandy in surprise, then slammed on the brakes. The car screeched to a halt less than ten yards from him.

Sandy turned without hesitation. He had to get out of the open. The patrolman would have to radio in his location before getting out of the car. That gave him an extra three seconds. He used it to run straight toward the six foot fence than ran along the sidewalk. He leapt up, grabbed the top and vaulted over into the backyard.

Then he crouched against the fence and waited.

It was a calculated risk. If the officer held his ground and radioed in his position, Sandy knew was probably screwed. Police would flood the area, set up a perimeter and bring in a K-9 for tracking. The K-9s were virtually foolproof if patrol set a hard perimeter. They'd come at him with the dog, a handler and a cover squad. Spokane had a progressive department, so he knew that patrol officers were issued long guns. That meant if he wanted to shoot it out with them, it would be his .45 versus their Colt AR-15s. Hardly a fair fight.

But it was still early enough in the morning that these officers were probably graveyard troops at the end of their shift. And graveyard troops tended to be more action-oriented than those on day shift. If the guy who spotted him was a high speed, low drag Type-A graveyard cop –

The fence rumbled and shook. A pair of hands grasped the top.

Sandy tensed.

The black clad officer swung over the fence and landed with a heavy thud.

Sandy waited another beat.

The officer took a step in the direction Sandy would have run, then slowed and turned back in his direction.

Sandy sprang at him.

He flashed out a left jab at the point of the cop's nose. The blow was weaker than he'd like, all arm but still stinging. He planted his feet and followed with a straight right. The punch crunched into the officer's left cheek and sent him staggering back. His radio fell to the ground. His eyes were dazed. He wavered on his feet.

Sandy didn't hesitate. He lashed out with his lead foot, landing it heavily in the groin. The officer grunted and dropped to his knees. Sandy stepped around his large frame and snaked his arm around the officer's neck. He compressed the sides, pressuring the carotid arteries. The officer flailed at him briefly with his hands, but all he could muster were weak slaps. A moment later, he succumbed to unconsciousness.

Sandy maintained the carotid hold for five more seconds. Then he let the officer slip to the ground as gently as he could. He grabbed the officer's gun and pulled, but it remained secure in the holster. Sandy examined the holster for a moment, recognized the security measure and withdrew the weapon. He threw the gun across the yard. Then he picked up the radio, released the battery pack and threw the two pieces in opposite directions.

Sirens filled the air. Sandy took a deep breath and launched himself at the fence again, scrambling over the top. His feet hit the pavement. He ran straight to the police car. The driver's door hung open and he slipped inside, hoping things hadn't changed radically in the twelve years since he'd driven a patrol cruiser. A laptop computer in the center console immediately dispelled that hope. He snapped it shut.

The control panel for the lights and siren was virtually the same as when he'd left the job. Sandy shut down the siren, leaving the overhead lights working. He pulled the door shut, dropped the car in gear and flipped a u-turn, heading in the opposite direction of the house.

The police radio blared with a mish-mash of voices announcing that they'd arrived on scene. A frenetic dispatcher tried to direct patrol units and relay information from the FBI. Sandy heard his name and description broadcast. He wondered how many of the responding officers would recognize him as a former brother.

He shut down the overhead lights and swung the patrol car in the direction of his Mazda. He heard no mention of his car on the police radio.

"Charlie-457?" the dispatcher asked.

There was no answer.

"Charlie-457, an update?"

No reply.

Sandy figured that Charlie-457 was the cop in the back yard. He'd be awake again by now, searching for his radio and his gun. If he didn't find it right away, he'd probably climb back over the fence and try to flag down another patrol unit.

"I need a unit to check on Charlie-457." The dispatcher put out the location. *"Last transmission, he had a possible suspect running southbound."*

"Charlie-453, got it. I'm ten seconds off."

"Copy."

Sandy pulled up to the curb just around the corner from his Mazda. He looked around the car for any equipment he could use. An AR-15 sat upright on the secure rack between the seats. In Sandy's day, that's where the shotgun was kept. He knew where the release button was and considered taking the gun. His .45 was miraculously still in his pouch pocket, but the rifle was a much better weapon.

He decided against it. He'd have to ditch the Mazda soon and unless he stole another car to replace it, there's no way he could conceal a rifle. Right now, stealth was his only hope. Firepower was not a priority.

Sandy turned off the patrol car. He left the keys in the ignition. He exited the vehicle and ran quickly around the corner and up to his Mazda, right where he'd left it. He got inside, started it up and backed smoothly out of the driveway. He dropped the car into gear and drove away south, away from the house.

As he drove, Sandy rolled down the window. He listened to the sirens. After a short while, the sirens stopped. That meant the area was sufficiently flooded with cops. He hoped that he was outside their perimeter. By now, he had no doubt that the officer had recovered and made contact with his fellows. They'd be looking for someone in a patrol car. That might buy him some time.

Sandy drove south at the speed limit until he hit the next arterial. Then he turned and drove along the arterial, heading into the business district. Traffic was still extraordinarily light. His heart was thudding in his ears as every car approached, wondering if it was a patrol cruiser. The FBI knew his car. They would put out a description soon, if they hadn't already.

Ahead on his left was a shopping center. Sandy signaled and pulled into the lot. Cars sparsely populated the parking spots, but that would change as employees arrived to work. Sandy found a small cluster of cars and slid into an empty stall in their midst. He cracked his window, then turned off the engine. He lowered his seat back until he was lying down.

He stared at the ceiling of the car. He would have to wait for the businesses to open. For more cars to get on the road. Then he would make his next move.

That would be several hours.

In the meantime, he had to think.

22

The strains of a Guns n' Roses guitar riff chimed out of the suit jacket on the passenger seat. He fished out the cell phone and flipped it open.

"Hey."

"Are you on scene yet?" she asked.

"Nope. Still about five minutes off. You?"

"The shift commander called me fifteen minutes ago. He's all in a twitter because of the inter-jurisdictional issues going on."

"What's the problem? It's a city homicide."

"The FBI is *always* a problem. I've already got a call from some asshole of a SAC telling me he was on his way to assume command of the crime scene."

"Fuck him. He has no jurisdiction."

"He *has* jurisdiction."

"How so?"

"Jesus, Lee. Federal agents, *his* agents, were involved in the shooting while investigating a federal case. If I were him, I'd be planting the flag, too."

He shook his head. "What the hell were federal agents doing following Banks?"

"I have no idea, but it scares the hell out of me."

He thought about it for a minute longer, mulling it over in his mind. If the feds were onto Sandy Banks, what else had they seen? Were they aware of the meeting he had with Banks at Brian's house? Were they up on Banks or the operation itself?

"Are you still there?" she asked.

"I'm here. Just thinking it through."

"Did you take care of the other loose end?"

"About an hour ago, yeah."

"Good."

Yeah, he thought. *If I wasn't followed.*

"We could be screwed," she said. He was surprised at how matter of fact her tone was. "If they're onto Banks, they might have had surveillance during the times you met with him."

"We'll know soon enough." He tried to project a confidence he wasn't sure he felt." I'll be on scene in a few minutes. I'll know by the questions they ask me if they're onto us."

"You know that they'll ask you where you were last night." Tension crept into her voice. "What are you going to say?"

"That I was fucking you."

"Goddamnit, Lee! I'm serious."

"Don't worry," he said, soothing her. 'I've got it covered. A buddy of mine will vouch for me staying with him."

"That won't hold up," she said. "Not if they start looking hard. Or if they push the guy."

"It will hold up," he assured her. "My guy won't break. And I won't lie about not being home. I'll even tell them that Kelly and I were having some marriage problems and that's why I wasn't there."

"Are you kidding me?" She sounded aghast. "Marriage problems? Talk about giving them a motive. Why don't you just confess to killing her?"

He smiled. "Baby, this ain't the 1950s. Marriage problems happen all the time. Husbands move out and stay with buddies. The couple either works it out or they don't. It doesn't add up to murder."

"It did in this case."

"But it doesn't in most." He paused, then said, "Listen, they'll look at it, yeah. They have to. But the life insurance on her isn't out of line. There's no other woman that they'll be aware of. My alibi will check out. Plus, the agents *saw* Banks. They'll know it wasn't me that did it."

"There's a lot of supposing going on in there, detective."

"Detective?" He pulled the phone away from his ear, cocking an eyebrow at it. Then he pressed it back to his ear. "Well, *Captain*, with all the command school training you've had, you know no plan survives contact with the enemy. We have to adapt and overcome. We knew that this would be the most difficult time."

She didn't reply.

"You also know," he continued, "that everything I just said has the absolute highest probability attached to it."

She sighed. "I do know. I'm just worried. If the feds—"

"If the feds know, we're fucked. So you stay away from the scene until I call you and let you know the coast is clear. If I don't call you in an hour, you need to get the hell out of Dodge."

"I'm the Captain of Detectives," she said. "It will look odd if I don't show up after I've been notified."

"Relax. It wasn't one of our officers involved in the shooting. Do your hair or something. No one will complain if the brass bitch takes her time getting on scene, anyway."

"I *hate* that name."

"Well, that's what they call you, baby. So make it work to your advantage. If I call you, show up and flex your captain's bars. Make that FBI SAC fight to own this crime scene. Maybe even win it for our guys."

"Fat chance of that."

He shrugged. "Maybe. If you're able to swing it, though, you should assign Jack Dorrance to the case."

"I was thinking Marty Hill."

"Nuh-uh. Hill's way too smart. He pulls at all the loose ends. You put him in there, he might actually *solve* the case. Let Dorrance work it. He'll cover enough bases along with the feds to put the murder on Banks and let the rest go unresolved."

"All right," she answered, her tone reluctant.

"Trust me, baby," he said. "I've been working around all these guys for ten years. I know what I'm talking about."

"I trust you."

"Good. After all the rigmarole at the scene, I'll have to do the bullshit family thing. So I'll meet you later."

"When?"

"Say nine-ish?"

"My place?"

"No. Too dangerous. Get a room at the Rutherford."

"The Rutherford? What's wrong with the motel we usually use?"

"Don't ever go back there," he said. "We don't want to risk it. Our faces are going to be plastered on the news. Especially mine." He smiled slightly. "Besides, the Rutherford is fancy. We can celebrate in style."

"Great. So tonight I'll either be in a luxury suite at the Rutherford or sitting in a jail cell."

"I gotta go, Linda," he said, ignoring her whining. "I'm just about there. I have to work up some tears of grief that will eventually slip through this tough cop exterior."

"Jesus, you're cold."

"Nah. I just let my warm and fuzzy self come out with you, that's all."

"That's the part of you that I love," she said. He thought he heard a catch in her voice.

"After all of this settles down, we'll be on easy street," he said.

"Right now, easy street seems a long ways away."

"It's just around the corner, baby," he assured her. "A few tough days and then it's a short term waiting game. I retire in grief, go ahead and get us set up down in the islands. A month later, you hang it up. It's a perfect plan."

"I thought you said no plan survives contact with the enemy."

"None do. But you gotta have a plan. And ours will work. Just stick with it."

"What about Banks?"

He laughed. "I wouldn't worry about Banks. City cops and the feds are looking for him. Hell, he just shot a federal agent. That's going to get him on their ten most wanted list for sure. He's got his hands full now."

She was quiet for a moment. Then she said, "Be careful."

"I will."

He snapped the phone shut and tossed it onto the passenger seat. Up ahead in the early dawn light, he could see the glow of blue and red police rotators. He needed to put on his game face.

Think of something sad.

His mind grasped for an idea that could bring tears to his eyes. All he could think of was the huge piles of money coming his way soon. True, his wife's life insurance policy wasn't big money, but it was a start. The real money would come from the sale of the big house on the South Hill that her rich daddy bought them outright as a wedding gift. That would net at least six hundred large, even with a quick sale by a 'motivated' seller. When you threw in whatever he could scavenge out of Kelly's half million dollar trust fund after sharing some with the kids, he would be set.

That only made him smile.

Losing all of that? Now *that* might make him cry.

23

Sandy remained lying back in the driver's seat. He'd gone over and over what he knew.

Brian was a snitch, working for the feds.

Odoms was untouchable, too much of a risk now.

The Keeper was a traitor.

And he'd murdered an innocent woman.

He stared at the car's ceiling, sorting through the mixture of emotions that came with those pieces of knowledge.

Disappointment. Rage. Guilt. They came over him in intermittent waves, none lasting long enough to gain a toehold before another emotion washed it aside.

His head hurt. He realized after a while that he was clenching his teeth so hard that it was causing the headache. Consciously, he forced himself to relax. The corners of his jaw immediately throbbed and ached when he stopped clenching his teeth. He reached up and rubbed the soreness with his thumb.

It doesn't matter what you feel, he told himself. *It matters what you do.*

There would be time enough for sorting out emotions later. Right now, his ass was on the line.

So what to do?

Sandy sat and listened as cars rolled past him. Engines cut out and doors slammed. Businesses were getting ready to open. He needed a plan.

Thoughts of revenge bubbled up, but he pushed them away. Revenge was a luxury he didn't have time for any more. He'd shot a federal agent. He would be on national teletypes now. He'd be lucky to stay out of custody.

He had to focus on escape.

His anger welled up again, seething in his chest. Most of it was directed at Larson. The son of a bitch manipulated him into murdering an innocent woman. He probably had some little spinner on the side and didn't want to lose half his retirement and that nice house in a divorce.

Brian, he could almost understand, as much as it galled him. The feds must have caught him somehow, so he cut a deal. It was a shitty thing to do, but at least it was out of some kind of survival. Sandy couldn't forgive him, but he couldn't work up enough of a desire for revenge to run the risk of searching him out. Not when Sandy was probably going to be on the ten most wanted list by noon today.

And Odoms? To hell with Odoms. He was just another scumbag who got away with it. He wasn't the first and wouldn't be the last. It wasn't Sandy's duty any more to do anything about it. Let karma take care of him. Or God, if there was one. It was out of Sandy's realm.

But Larson? That one burned him. He liked to believe he wasn't a vengeful person by nature, though that thought was laughable whenever he took an objective look at what he'd been doing for the past twelve years. But that had been his destiny. He'd known it since he was fifteen. He had penance to pay. When Cal Ridley bailed him out of the jackpot he was in and made him a Horseman, he figured that was simply karma giving him a second chance to make good.

Or maybe God.

Sandy let out a small snort of disgust. Didn't most crazy people who commit murders come to believe that they are an instrument of God at some point? Maybe he'd reached that summit. Hell, maybe he was over the rise.

"Maybe you need to focus," he said aloud in a low voice.

His mind clicked through all the possibilities, and he kept coming back to the simple answer: Larson was a luxury he couldn't afford.

Escape. That was his mission.

Sandy eased the driver's seat forward into an upright position. Cars were scattered throughout the parking lot. Foot traffic was light, but he felt safe enough to get out of the car. Besides, eventually cops would be cruising parking lots, looking for this car. He'd pushed his luck far enough.

He pulled his sweatshirt over his head, leaving the .45 in the pouch pocket. The belt that he wore underneath would look odd to even a casual onlooker, so he unbuckled it, rolled it up and put it on top of the sweatshirt. He dug around in the glove compartment and found the emergency twenty dollar bill he kept in there. Grabbing the folded sweatshirt, he exited the car. He tossed the keys on the driver's floor, locked the door and closed it.

He glanced around the parking lot. He spotted a second hand clothing shop tucked in between a used bookstore and a health food store. Twenty bucks ought to be enough for a change of clothes. He walked purposefully toward the shop. Once inside, he dug around in a bin full of jeans until he found his size. Then he flipped through the hanging shirts, finally settling on a tan flannel that was a size too large. That made for a grand total of six dollars and forty two cents. He splurged, spending eight-fifty on a battered pair of construction boots.

At the register, the clerk was a forty-ish woman that looked slightly retarded. Sandy looked around for a manager but no one else was in the store.

"Hello," she said, her voice tinged with that particular

deepness he always associated with Down's syndrome.

"Hello," Sandy replied.

The woman laboriously added the three items and gave Sandy a total. He handed her the twenty. She slowly made change, then gave him a cherub-like smile. "Thank you for giving us your business," she said in a practiced tone.

"You're welcome," Sandy answered. "Hey, I bought these for work today. Can I change into them here?"

She gave him a slightly confused look, then shrugged. "Okay." She pointed at the changing room in the back of the store.

Sandy smiled at her. "Thanks."

He made his way to the rear of the store. Quickly, he shed his sweat pants and dressed in the boots, jeans and flannel. He kept his T-shirt on and left the flannel untucked, slipping the .45 into his belt underneath it. He looked in the mirror. The flannel hung loosely, concealing the weapon.

Sandy walked out of the store, giving the cashier a neutral nod. Once he was around the corner, he found a trash can. He deposited the sweats inside.

He checked his pocket. He had five dollars and change. That was enough for the bus.

But where to?

He couldn't go home. The feds and the cops would be all over that location. And if Brian had flipped, the safe house they had set aside was burnt. So was the office. Anything that any of the Horsemen or the Keeper knew about was now dangerous ground.

He needed cash. That was first. He had some money and false IDs hidden in a wooded area outside of town. But the more he moved around right now, the greater chance someone would spot him. He needed to lie low for a while.

Cal, he thought. The old lieutenant had set up an out for each of the Horsemen in the event that the operation was compromised. But Cal was gone and George Larson obviously wasn't his ticket out of town.

Sandy walked casually toward the nearest bus stop, realizing that he'd just made his decision. He'd go to Gail. Maybe Cal had a lock box or a safe with an escape plan and documents still inside. If nothing else, he felt sure that Gail would let him stay there until the heat died down. Then he could find his own way out.

He took a seat in the enclosed bus stop and waited.

24

"**Y**ou two sure made a mess of things," he said.

Special Agent Lori Carter glanced up from her hands. She'd been staring at the dried blood on her fingers for several hours now, watching as it faded quickly from the bright red that had flowed out of McNichol's thigh. As she sat worrying in the hospital waiting room, the red became darker until now it was quite black. In the midst of all the clamor at the scene and then here at the hospital, it never occurred to her to wash it off.

When she looked up, she was met by the pinched, condescending expression of her Special Agent-in-Charge, Edward Maw.

Her mouth was open and the wrong words just about spilled out before she caught herself. She snapped her lips shut and exhaled, searching for something to say that would be the right thing but wouldn't make her feel like a serf.

Maw seemed to take delight in her dilemma. "The scene back there is a mess. I just spent the last hour fending off some Medusa of a city police captain who wanted to lay claim to the investigation. And Banks is still unaccounted for."

"He'll turn up," Carter said.

Maw's eyebrows shot up. "He'll turn up? That's the best you can do?"

"Sorry," she snapped. "I'm a little worried about my partner here."

Maw pursed his lips, then nodded. "Yes, of course. How *is* Agent McNichol, anyway?"

"In surgery."

"Still?"

Carter nodded, looking down at her bloody hands. "It was a femoral artery hit."

Maw let out a low whistle. "That's too bad."

She looked up at him in amazement. "That's too bad?" she repeated. "What planet are you from?"

Maw scowled. "I'm a professional, Agent Carter. I recognize that there is a danger associated with field operations. While it is sad when an agent is injured or killed, it is always a possibility. It doesn't negate our responsibility to continue with the mission."

Carter opened her mouth to reply, but he interjected before she had a chance.

"And I am also your superior officer, Agent Carter. Let's not forget that."

"Little chance of that," Carter replied, her tone as neutral as she could muster.

Maw's scowl deepened. "I'm going to forgive your insubordination due to the obvious stress of the situation. But don't test the limits of my generosity."

Carter felt her face flush. She clenched her jaw to hold in a retort. She balled her hands into fists at her sides to resist throttling the officious prick standing over her.

I should stand up, she thought. *Not let him tower over me.*

Maw watched her silently.

She took in a breath, then two. She thought about standing, then rejected the idea.

Forget it. Who cares?

"The vic was a cop's wife," she finally said, changing the

subject.

"I know."

"Are we looking at the husband?"

"Of course."

"Does he make?"

Maw shook his head. "Probably not. They were having some minor marital discord, but nothing severe. And his alibi has already been confirmed."

"Maybe he hired Banks," Carter suggested.

Maw smirked at her. "Unlikely. Banks goes after criminals who have skirted the system. The victim was a civilian."

"What if the husband could be involved in the Horseman operation?" Carter theorized. "He could manipulate things so that—"

"Doubtful," Maw interrupted.

"Why?"

"Moore said that he was recruited by Banks, right?"

"Yes, but that could be bullshit."

Maw frowned at her profanity. "His life is on the line. I hardly think he would lie in that instance."

"Liars lie," Carter said.

"Nevertheless," Maw said dismissively, "Detective Merchant wasn't even a detective at the time Banks left the police department. He was still a patrol officer. Whoever has been feeding information to Banks and the other Horsemen has to be a higher ranking officer. Or perhaps a civilian."

"Why higher ranking?"

"It's sensitive business," Maw said. "You can't expect line personnel to carry that off for a dozen years."

"No, of course not," she said, barely masking her sarcasm.

Maw ignored her tone. "My theory remains that it is a judge or someone in the court system. That's the most likely scenario."

"It still doesn't explain why Banks would target a civilian."

"If you and Agent McNichol had apprehended him," Maw replied, his own voice cut with sarcasm, "we could ask Banks that very question."

Carter pressed her lips together and swallowed the reply that had flashed through her mind. Instead, she said, "This isn't random. There has to be a reason for Banks to do this."

"And I believe that when we discover who the Keeper is, that reason will be self-evident."

Carter shrugged. "It could be that our snitch is lying and there is no Keeper. Maybe the Horsemen just do their own research. With the Internet and public disclosure laws, it wouldn't be that difficult."

"I suppose we'll see when we get the forensics back on Banks's computer," Maw said. "But I don't think so."

"You executed the warrant on his apartment already?"

Maw nodded. "And on the storage unit with all the files. I ordered it as soon as I realized that you compromised the operation."

"Compromised? Sir, it was a matter of life or death."

"Perhaps," Maw said.

"There was no perhaps about it. He—"

"If that rationalization makes you more comfortable with your actions, Agent Carter, then by all means cling to it." He smiled humorlessly. "But we both know that you violated protocol when you broke surreptitious surveillance."

"Protocol?" She shook her head. "Did you really just say that?"

"I did."

"You're kidding me."

Maw shook his head. "Not at all. Your assignment was surveillance only. You were not authorized to engage the target absence extraordinary exigence. But we'll discuss this at greater length when things are under more control."

Carter took a deep breath before speaking. She'd stopped

caring about this case. All that mattered was seeing her partner through. "I plan on staying here until Scott's stabilized and awake," she said. "After that—"

"I'm giving you twelve hours for that and to get some sleep," Maw interrupted. "After that, report to me for your next assignment."

Carter frowned. "You're putting me with another team for the rest of this investigation?"

He shook his head. "No. I'm transferring you to an administrative position."

She gawked at him. "An admini—" She stopped, then said, "You're joking."

"Joking would not be appropriate, given the situation," Maw said. "You blew this case, Agent Carter. Your field days in this office are done."

She shook her head at him. "You…you…"

"Careful," he said. "Or your career at the Bureau will be the next thing to go."

Carter stared at him in disbelief. "Now? You're telling me this now? While Scott is in there fighting for his life?"

"As I explained, the world marches on," Maw told her. He glanced at his watch. "Call me to check in at 2200 hours." He turned to go, then stopped and pointed at her lap. "And wash your hands. That's disgusting."

Carter didn't reply. She watched Maw stalk from the waiting room. Then she resumed staring down at her blood-blackened hands.

25

Sandy got off the bus several blocks from Gail Ridley's house. He approached cautiously, taking a seat on a park bench up the street and watching for a full hour before he felt sure there was no surveillance.

As he sat and watched, he let the events of the past day rattle around inside his head. He relived his last conversation with Brian in his mind, hearing his words in a different light.

Sorry, Sandy.

I hate doing this to you.

I just don't feel like I have a choice anymore.

Sandy reflected again on the strong likelihood that Brian had been wearing a wire that day. He tried to think about his own replies. What had he said? How incriminating had they been?

He shook his head. It didn't matter now. Shooting Kelly Caper this morning was enough to earn him the death penalty. If the federal agent he'd shot died, too, that sealed things. Brian's testimony would merely be icing on the cake.

Sandy pushed those thoughts away. They had to catch him for that to matter, and he didn't plan on being caught. Still, he wondered how much Brian had told the feds when he flipped. Did he say anything about Cal? Or did he just pretend to be in the dark about the nuts and bolts of the operation? Hell, he could have passed Sandy off as the mastermind of the whole thing.

But if he mentioned Cal, investigators would eventually think to contact Gail. Probably sooner rather than later.

If he hadn't, her house was safe.

Sandy replayed his last conversation with Brian, trying to recall as many details as he could. Had they talked about Cal?

He was almost sure of it.

So was Gail's house safe, after all?

Sandy worked through the question in his mind. Even if they knew about Cal, they knew he'd been dead for a decade. Would they even have thought about his widow? They couldn't suspect her of being part of the project, so why would they?

No, Sandy figured. Gail's house was safe from the Feds.

Larson knew about Gail, though. He'd been there once before. Would he come back now, looking for Sandy?

Sandy scratched the stubble on his chin. Larson wouldn't be looking for him, he realized. He'd done Larson's dirty work, for whatever reason the Keeper wanted it done. He probably hoped Sandy disappeared forever.

Forget Larson for now, he told himself.

Focus.

He needed a place to lay up, at least until dark. Gail was his best bet. And if Cal had a safe or a lock box, it might contain a better out than his own that he could use.

He made his decision. He rose from the park bench and headed up the street toward the small residence. No one passed him on the short walk.

As he approached the front door, he could see that the curtains were drawn. A faint flicker of light from the television danced behind them. Sandy pulled open the screen door and knocked.

No response.

He waited for a full thirty seconds before knocking again,

this time louder.

Still no response.

Maybe she wasn't home, he thought. Maybe Cal taught her to leave the TV on to discourage any burglars.

Burglars like he was about to become.

Sandy closed the screen door. He made his way around the house, trying to look into windows without appearing suspicious. All of the curtains were closed. In his mind, he rationalized what he was about to do.

Cal would approve. Especially after what Larson had become.

Gail won't care. She'll want to help.

He needed the place to hide until he could get out of town under cover of darkness.

Even though each of those thoughts rang true, he still had a queasy feeling in his stomach. Gail trusted him. She let him into her home, shared her Bailey's and coffee and confided in him. Now he was going to violate that trust. It was something he had to do, but he still didn't feel good about it.

At the back door, Sandy examined the lock. He frowned. No doubt Cal had been security conscious, but he must have passed that trait to his wife as well. The lock and deadbolt were less than three years old and designed to thwart lock-picking and brute force alike.

He crouched, reaching for the lock picks strapped to his ankle. The only thing approximating a window in the door were three narrow glass strips. Behind those hung sheer curtains with some sort of floral design. With the angle of the light, Sandy could see through the glass.

On the ground, he saw the shadowy form of two legs extending into the kitchen from the living room.

He blinked.

It was Gail. Had to be. She must have had a heart attack or something and fallen down.

How long ago?

As he stared through the glass, he saw her foot twitch.

Sandy reacted without thinking. He stood, stepped back and delivered a forceful kick to the door right next to the knob. The wood in the jamb cracked and splintered. The door flew open.

Sandy charged in, his mind whirring through possibilities, through plans.

I have to save her.

Call 911.

Perform CPR until the medics get here. Let them take over and slip away before the cops arrive.

Sandy barreled through the kitchen and around the corner to Gail before the coppery scent registered in his nostrils.

Gail lay on her back, her jaw slack. Her arms were splayed out to the side like fragile wings. Expressionless eyes stared up at the ceiling. A dark, sticky mass of blood matted her hair and the surrounding carpet. The light from the television flickered and jumped on her still frame, giving the illusion of movement.

"Jesus," Sandy whispered. He felt the strength go out of his legs. Instead of resisting it, he sank to his knees.

Tears prickled his eyes.

"Oh, Gail," he whispered.

The tears threatened, but he forced them away, driving the emotion down deep inside. Instead, he latched onto something else. Something that he'd barely been able to hold in abeyance since he stood in that hallway after shooting an innocent woman.

Rage.

"Larson," Sandy said aloud, his voice still thick.

He knew it was him, as sure as if there'd been a bloody footprint of a wingtip shoe on display like a signature. Gail knew about him and about the Horseman. She was a loose end and Larson had cleaned it up.

"You son of a bitch," Sandy said, staring down at Gail's impassive expression. "You just changed my plans."

26

Sandy closed the back door. Then he rummaged around in the hall closet until he found a dark blanket. He draped it over the upper half of Gail Ridley. He knew it was the wrong thing to do from a crime scene perspective, but didn't care. The woman had been a kind soul. She deserved her dignity.

He stood over the shrouded form, struggling for a moment. It had been a long time since he'd stood next to a dead body that had belonged to someone that he cared for. Hell, outside of Brian and the other Horsemen, it had been a long time since he'd had the opportunity to care about anyone at all. Most of the time, when there was a dead body in the room, he was busy making sure it looked accidental or like a suicide.

This was different. This was Cal's wife. And Cal had been good to him. So had Gail. She deserved something more than an old blanket for a shroud.

Sandy cleared his throat. He wasn't sure if he believed in God anymore, but he wasn't sure that he didn't, either. So he spoke half-remembered phrases from long ago services.

"The Lord is your Shepherd, Gail," he muttered.

The ticking of the clock on the mantelpiece seemed as loud as a church bell.

"Give us this day our daily bread," he said.

When was the last time he'd been in a church?

Not Cal's death.

None of the line of duty deaths while he was on the job, either. He'd always volunteered to cover shifts so others could go.

"Ashes to ashes," he said.

There'd been the military funerals. Sparsely attended. Complete with the lies that the family members were told to cover for operations that were never acknowledged.

"Dust to dust."

Lies that he had to repeat and endure. Lies from another life.

"Our Father…"

Images of a huge church flashed in his mind. His own feet dangling over the seat of the pew. His mother weeping. His own confusion. Daddy had left for work one morning, just like all the others. How could he be in that long box at the front of the church? He'd risen from the breakfast table and walked out of the kitchen, tousling Sandy's hair as he swept past. The ever-present odor of machinist's oil wafted over Sandy as he sat at that kitchen table, nursing his oatmeal and glass of milk. He couldn't remember his father's kisses, if they ever occurred, but he remembered that strong, masculine smell on his hands and clothing. As the years passed, he remembered it better even than his father's face.

"Hallowed be thy name…"

And then a decade later. Standing in the back of that same church. His mother's picture next to the inexpensive casket. The priest's empty words assuring everyone in the building that even though this same fate awaited them, too, there was hope. Always hope.

That was the first time he felt true rage. Rage for the false promises he believed the clergyman was spewing out next to the body of his dead mother. Rage for the step-father who finally took his "discipline" too far. Rage at himself for finally doing something about it after it was too late to matter.

That day, in that same church, he'd been unable to remain until the last blessings were spoken over her. He left, carrying all of the weight of her death with him. Over and over, the same thought burned in his mind and in his chest.

I should have stopped him.

I failed her.

The story of his life.

"Forgive us our trespasses, as we forgive—" he stopped, choking on the final words. He swallowed the sadness. Used it to fuel his anger.

He looked down at Gail again. He wondered if she would want vengeance for her death. Maybe she would have it in her heart somehow to forgive.

Sandy knew Cal wouldn't.

He took a deep breath and shook his head.

No, there were plenty of people willing to forgive. Sandy was not one of them.

George Larson was a dead man.

"Amen," he said over Gail's still form.

He searched the house methodically, always keeping an ear open. If someone saw him boot the door, they'd have called police. After thirty minutes, he felt confident that no one had seen him and that the police weren't coming.

There wasn't a safe anywhere on the main floor. Sandy checked everywhere. Behind pictures. In the closets, including on the floor for a buried safe. Nothing.

On the top shelf in the bedroom, he found a small metal box. The three digit combination lock was barely more than a privacy lock. He pried it open with a screwdriver. A small wad of cash and a stack of black and white wedding pictures fell to the floor.

Carefully, he picked up the photographs. He arranged

them neatly in a stack and put them back into the box. Then he picked up the money. A quick count revealed four hundred dollars, all in twenty dollar bills.

A careful sweep of the basement revealed nothing. No safe, no lockbox, nothing in any of the storage trunks. If Cal had kept an out, he'd hidden it too well for Sandy to find.

Back upstairs, he averted his eyes from the covered form of Gail's body as he walked past. Four hundred dollars would be enough, he hoped. It would have to be. And he'd have to risk being out in the open again, because he couldn't stay here any longer. Maybe the police would discover him, maybe they wouldn't. But he couldn't intrude upon Gail's home any more than he already had.

He slipped out the back door and headed back to the bus stop.

He rode the bus longer than he wanted to, but it was the only way to avoid the central bus station. He doubted the cops would search every single bus, but he was pretty sure that security at the main terminal would have been advised of his description. They might even post an officer down there to monitor security cameras. The city buses went all the way out to the college in Cheney, where someone could catch a Greyhound bus without going to the main Intermodal train and bus station. The police would want to cover that central station.

He changed buses three times before getting off in the East Sprague district. Every city had a place like East Sprague. It was the "down there" of Spokane. Prostitutes were thick, drugs were available and there were as many stolen property fences as there were legitimate businesses.

No one asked questions down here, Sandy knew. He could pay cash for a room in a dive motel without arousing suspicion.

The tradeoff was that East Sprague was heavily patrolled by police. He risked being spotted. With computers in the patrol cars, he was certain his picture had been disseminated to every patrol officer. Finding him had to be a high priority.

Sandy walked down the sidewalk, not meeting anyone's eye but being careful not to let that avoidance be apparent. He ignored the offer of a prostitute on the first corner. As soon as he crossed the street, someone from a darkened doorway asked him, "You lookin'?"

He ignored that as well and kept walking.

Half a block ahead, he saw a sign for Palm d'Or motel. The 'm' was burnt out and the large 'O' flickered, but in the late afternoon light, the sign was still easy enough to read. Sandy made for it.

In his peripheral vision, he caught sight of a white car. As it rolled further past him, the red and blue lights on top came into view. Sandy tensed inside. He wanted to reach for his .45, still tucked in his belt under the flannel, but he knew better. If he acted suspiciously, they'd key on him. Then they'd recognize him from the picture he was sure they had on the computer. Then it was the gunfight at O.K. Corral. He'd already killed one innocent woman and maybe a federal agent. Shooting more cops was not something he wanted to do.

The police car slowed.

Sandy clenched his teeth.

The lights came on suddenly.

Sandy reached for his gun.

The tires chirped. The engine roared and the car shot down Sprague toward some other emergency.

Sandy relaxed slightly. The city never shuts down, he realized, no matter what else happens.

He crossed the small parking lot to the office of the Palm d'Or motel. A small man with a buzz cut sat at the desk, watching a movie on a tiny television. His nametag read Arlo.

He looked up from eating sunflower seeds.

"Do for ya?" Arlo asked, spitting shells into the trash can between his legs.

"I need a room."

"Hourly or for the night?"

"For the night."

"Forty bucks." He pushed a card toward Sandy. "Fill out the registration card. No pets. No loud parties. And I need a credit card in the case of damages."

Sandy peeled off two twenties and put them on the counter. Then he peeled off another and laid it on top of the registration card. Arlo eyed the money, then looked at Sandy. Sandy met his eyes with a neutral gaze.

"That take care of the deposit?"

Arlo spat out another shell. Without a word, he took the twenty and slipped it into his pocket. He grabbed a key and handed it to Sandy. "Number thirteen," he said. Then he smiled, showing a blackened front tooth. "Mr. Smith."

Sandy nodded his thanks, left the office and headed for the room. Once inside, he found a tiny space with a double bed, an aged television and a bathroom of questionable cleanliness. He shrugged. It wasn't what he was used to, but he'd been in worse places.

Images of sleeping in the desert in what looked like a shallow grave sprang to mind. He pushed the thought away, but visions of a single wide trailer replaced it.

"Stop it," he muttered.

He'd done a good job running from his past, and paying penance for it. There was no time to wallow in either one right now.

Focus on the mission, soldier.

Find Larson. Eliminate Larson. Get out of town and disappear.

Sandy slid the only chair in the place in front of the door, propping it under the knob. Then he settled onto the bed, turned on the television and waited for darkness.

27

He stepped out onto the back porch of his daughter's house, ostensibly to be alone. After a backwards glance to make sure no one was watching him, he dumped the rest of the drink he'd been nursing onto the grass. Let them think he was drowning his sorrows over their poor mother. They probably expected it, but he needed to keep his head straight.

He tugged at his already loosened tie and sighed. Another couple of hours, he figured, and then he could come up with some reason to leave. It wasn't like he was close with his kids anyway. If he stayed too long, that reality would overshadow the tragedy of the day.

Then it was off to the Rutherford.

He smiled.

His cell phone vibrated. He pulled it from his jacket pocket and examined the incoming phone number. His smile widened and he flipped it open.

"Zack," he said.

"Lee." Zack's voice was its usual monotone. "How's it going?"

"Peachy," he said. "You call bearing gifts?"

"Yeah, sorta. I did the work up for you on Sandy Banks."

"And?"

"And it's goofy."

He frowned. "Goofy how?

"Like, as in strange."

"He doesn't have a military record?"

"No, he has a record. There's a file, but it's thin. Way too thin. There's just a little basic information and his DD-214."

"English, Zack."

"Sorry. A DD-214 is his discharge paperwork."

"So what's strange about that?"

"I've just never seen such a vanilla personnel record before. It only has a few basic sheets in here besides his DD…er, his discharge papers. None of the usual stuff that finds its way into these files."

"Like what?"

"Like transfer orders, physical fitness tests, performance reviews, promotional letters, awards, stuff like that."

"He doesn't have that stuff?"

"Nope."

"So maybe Banks was a low achiever," he suggested.

"Maybe. Or his record was lost somehow and had to be recreated later. That was my first thought. On account of how any of the paperwork that has writing on it is all in the same hand."

"You said that was your first thought?"

"Yeah. But that's not the case. I did a little checking. I called to the two different units where Banks served during his enlistment. I talked to my counterparts in both of those units. They had no record of Banks."

"Should they?"

"Absolutely. In fact, they'd have more background information on him than we do here at Central Files."

"So you're telling me that the file you're holding right now is fake?"

"I'd say so, yeah. And I'd be willing to bet that this DD-214 is what Banks used to get hired by the police department out there."

He thought about that. Department of Licensing would probably accept military discharge papers and a military ID to get a driver's license. And the police department was full of ex-military. No one would question discharge papers and a driver's license. They'd hire the guy and then issue him a department identification card. With a police ID and a driver's license, he'd be a shoe-in to create a complete identity.

"Is there a birth certificate?" he asked.

"Nope. That's the other thing that jumped out at me. There are three things every file should have in it and a birth certificate is one of them."

"What are the other two?"

"Enlistment papers and discharge papers," Zack told him. "That's what's most important to the Army, Lee. That you were born, that you joined the military and that you were discharged. Everything else is just details."

"So what you're telling me is—"

"What I'm telling you is that this guy you're investigating may have been in the Army, but he sure as hell *isn't* Sergeant Sandy Banks. Sandy Banks is a ghost."

He was quiet for a moment, thinking. Then he asked, "How could someone do this? How do they get away with it?"

"The Army is the biggest corporation in the world," Zack said. "There are mounds of paper generated just to buy a box of toothpicks. It's easy to hide things in all that."

"But someone would have to want to do it. And have the connections to make it happen."

"True," Zack admitted. "But there's any number of people that could handle that."

"Do you suppose he was some kind of Special Forces or something?"

"Coulda been, yeah. But he could've been some First Sergeant's kid who had a dishonorable discharge or something and needed clean papers for a fresh start. Who knows?"

"Thanks, Zack. I owe you."

"Nah. Happy to help an old buddy whose one of the good guys."

"I appreciate it."

"Take care, Lee. And let me know what you figure out about this guy. I'm curious now."

"I will. Bye."

He disconnected and stared down at the phone for a few moments before putting it away. He couldn't shake the feeling of surprise. He'd expected to hear something along the lines of combat training for Banks, or even some battlefield experience. But this was something else entirely.

Sandy Banks did not exist.

So who the hell was the guy he set up?

He wondered briefly if he had bitten off more than he could chew. Normally, he wouldn't entertain such a ridiculous thought, but the shadowy nature of Banks' past worried him.

His next thought was, should he tell Linda?

He considered the question. That immediately begged the obvious follow-up: could he still trust her?

Sure, he could, he decided. She loved him. That was obvious. He supposed he loved her, too, though he wondered how much of that was really love and how much was the fact that she'd been his ticket out of the mess he was in.

He let out a weary sigh. He'd started sleeping with her more on a lark than anything. Imagine being able to tell the guys in the bullpen that he nailed the Brass Bitch? Their boss's boss's boss? That would have been a definite boost to his reputation, even with those guys on the job who were big time trim hounds.

Then it changed a little for him. He wasn't sure how exactly or even when, but it did. It felt a little different than the others. He found himself thinking about her more. Not just sexual fantasies, but imagining a life alone with her. Away from all of the bullshit.

He blamed his head in the clouds state of mind for getting sloppy. Kelly got suspicious, which was nothing new. This time, though, she found small pieces of evidence. A receipt that was clearly dinner for two. She didn't buy his argument that it was his partner.

"Your partner wears lipstick?" she'd snapped at him, holding up his shirt, rescued from the laundry.

He tried everything he could, following the age-old methods of cheaters everywhere. He admitted nothing. He denied everything. He tried to counter-accuse, even though he knew it was a lame tactic with no teeth. Then he resorted to calling her paranoid and crazy.

"We'll see how paranoid I am in divorce court," she told him. "We'll see how crazy things are when I have half your pension and you're living in some lousy apartment somewhere. See if your whore girlfriend is impressed with that."

"Kell—"

"Everything is mine, Lee," she'd told him. "It's all in my name. You'll get nothing. Do you understand? Not a thing."

And he knew she was right.

He had to smile now, in spite of everything. He smiled because although she'd been right at the time, she sure as hell wasn't right anymore.

The door behind him opened. His daughter leaned out of the doorway. "You okay, Dad?"

He cleared his throat and feigned wiping tears away before turning around. "Fine," he said.

She glanced down at the empty glass in his left hand, then back up at him. She tried to conceal her disapproval. "Coming inside?" she asked.

He nodded. "Yeah. In a minute."

"Okay," she said. She stood watching him for a moment. Then she added, "You look like you have the weight of the world on you, Dad."

He looked down into his glass as if he didn't know where the liquor went. "Still adjusting to the shock of everything," he said.

She opened the door wide for him. "Come inside. Be with family."

"All right," he said.

For a few more hours or so, he thought.

28

Sandy watched the news broadcast carefully. The police and the FBI were being surprisingly close-mouthed about the shooting. The reporters only talked about the barest details. Unfortunately, that included a fairly good description of him. The name of the victim was not mentioned.

He flipped to another local channel. This reporter was mid-way through his story.

"Officials are not releasing the names of the wounded agent or the homicide victim. However, investigative journalists here at KRDQ have uncovered the following exclusive information: the residence where the homicide occurred is owned by Lee and Kelly Merchant. Now, since the victim in this shooting is being reported by police as being female, there is speculation that it is, in fact, Mrs. Kelly Merchant."

Kelly Merchant, Sandy thought. *Now I know who I murdered.*

"An interesting side note," the reporter continued, "is that Lee Merchant, who we assume is the deceased's husband, is a local police detective."

And now I know who George Larson really is.

"Here is the scene earlier today, where Detective Merchant was comforted by his co-workers." The picture cut away from the reporter to file footage of the man Sandy knew as George Larson standing outside the house. Tears streamed down his cheeks. A fellow detective had his hand on Larson's—no, *Merchant's* shoulder. A moment later, a woman in a business suit exited the house. She reached out and gave Merchant a hug. His hands moved to the small of her back, hovered, then settled there.

Sandy's eyes narrowed.

A moment later, the video cut away to that same woman in mid-sentence. "—and so we will cooperate fully and assist the FBI in any way we can with this investigation."

Below her, subtitles announced her identity.

Investigative Captain Linda Valczinski.

An off-camera voice asked her, "Why is the FBI taking lead on a city homicide?"

Captain Valczinski didn't miss a beat. "I can't comment on that. This is their investigation."

The video snapped back to the field reporter. "The FBI also refused to comment, other than to confirm that the suspect is still at large and should be considered armed and dangerous. Back to you, Mandy."

A perfectly coiffed anchorwoman appeared on screen. "Thank you, Alan. Tonight, the school district superintendent announced a cut in –"

Sandy turned off the television.

He ran through the video in his mind. Watched that hug over and over again. Saw her step into his embrace. Saw the hand fall to the small of her back.

There was something wrong with it.

But what?

After a few minutes, he knew.

It was too familiar. Merchant hadn't held onto her like a bereaved husband might hold a colleague.

He'd held her like a lover.

Sandy considered the thought. It was an awfully big leap to make just from a few moments of video. A police captain sleeping with one of her detectives? It didn't seem likely. Not in today's age of hyper-vigilance when it came to sexual harassment and workplace ethics.

Still, whenever he replayed that touch in his mind, there was less and less doubt in his mind. The way Merchant's hand found its way so comfortably to the small of her back? They were lovers.

Sandy struggled with the internal argument for a few minutes. Finally, he conceded that while it was a long shot, he didn't have many options. And if Valczinski and Merchant were lovers, there was only one way to find out.

Sandy rose and opened the single drawer in the nightstand. Under a bible was a telephone book. He pulled it out and flipped through it, looking through the Vs.

No Valczinski.

"You didn't really think it would be that easy, did you?" he muttered to himself.

He glanced up at the clock. Almost five-fifteen. The libraries should be open until nine.

Sandy left the motel room and headed down to see Arlo, hoping that the clerk didn't watch the news.

"A car?" Arlo squinted at him.

"For a day or so."

Arlo spit out a sunflower shell. "I can loan you mine for a hundred bucks."

Sandy didn't hesitate. He pulled out his money and counted off five twenties.

"You got a driver's license?"

Sandy stopped. "Yes. Why?"

"Cops'll tow the car if you get stopped without a license. I don't want to have to pay to get the car out of impound."

Sandy nodded in understanding. "No problem. My license

is valid."

"Show me."

Sandy paused. "I don't have it with me."

Arlo shook his head. "Forget it, then. It'll cost me a hundred bucks just to get it out of impound."

"They'll check my name," Sandy said. "It'll come back with a good license."

"Uh-uh."

Sandy sighed. He counted off another hundred dollars. "This is a deposit against an impound, all right? When I bring the car back, you give it back. If it gets impounded, you're still ahead a hundred bucks. All right?"

Arlo eyed the money for a moment. Then he shrugged and snapped up the bills. He fished a pair of keys out of his jeans pocket. "It's the green Ford Maverick out front. Bring it back with the same amount of gas in it." He tossed the keys to Sandy.

Sandy caught them. "Thanks," he said, and left.

The Hillyard branch of the library was quiet. One of the librarians looked up at Sandy as he entered and smiled. Sandy nodded back, then headed straight for the computers before she asked him if he had a library card.

He sat down at a computer and brought up a web browser. The default page was the library home page. He navigated away to a search engine. Then he typed in "Linda Valczinski."

He got seven hits. All seven were about a Polish gymnast.

He revised his search to "Linda Valczinski Spokane."

Only four hits this time. The second one was a DIREC-TORY/PEOPLE site. He clicked on that. The first listing was the only one that matched in Spokane. He read off the address.

2731 South Latawah.

He wanted to shake his head at how easy it was, but the last few years of researching targets had taken the surprise out of how much information was available on the Internet. There was no such thing as true privacy anymore.

Just to be certain, he ran the address through the county tax assessor's office. The record for that year came back to Linda Valczinski. The photograph showed a small brick bungalow that sat back off the street deep into the lot. He examined the layout of the doors and windows. A side door on the garage side. The garage sat slightly behind.

He clicked on the search engine's MAP function and entered the address. Once the arrow was centered on the address, he switched to satellite view. Now he had a scrolling picture of the entire block. He navigated left and right. About two houses away and on the opposite side of the street, he spotted a huge weeping willow that hung over the street.

Perfect.

Sandy switched to the police department website. He found an entry for Captain Linda Valczinski, which listed a very brief bio. There was no mention of a husband. He stared at her formal photograph, taken in full uniform. She was a moderately attractive woman, he admitted, but her plastic smile bothered him. He could see the cold calculation in her eyes. It was as if, at the moment the camera flashed, she was trying to determine how much and what kind of advantage she could get out of that smile.

Her and Larson, Sandy thought. *Two peas in a pod.*

Then he shook his head.

Merchant, he told himself. His name is Detective Lee Merchant. Larson was the alias that he used with Gail. An alias that would work fine to cover his tracks for a while, at least until she saw his picture on the television news. That's why he came back and –

Sandy ground his teeth together and swallowed thickly.

He clicked away from the website, not wanting to look to see if there was a grinning picture of Lee Merchant or not. He was too sure that there was.

He sat at the terminal for a few moments, his mind clicking off possibilities. He asked himself about the likelihood of a police captain and a detective having an affair. It seemed unlikely. Still, he'd seen the embrace on television. He knew enough about human behavior to recognize it for what it was – a lover's touch.

So did Captain Valczinski know about the Horsemen? Or that Merchant was the Keeper? Or was she guilty of nothing more than adultery?

Sandy thought again of that cold, calculating smile and shook his head.

No, he figured. She was in it up to her eyeballs.

Still, all of this was conjecture. There was only one way to know for sure.

Sandy stood to leave, then hesitated. On a whim, he typed another entry into the search engine. The best he could find was a general number for what he wanted, but he supposed it would be enough. He jotted that number down next to the address on the slip of paper beside the keyboard. Then he rose and left the library without meeting anyone's gaze.

Outside, he called the number at a corner payphone. The operator was very helpful. He jotted the phone number down on the back of his hand, thanked her and hung up.

29

Special Agent Lori Carter watched her partner's eyelids flutter. She took a shallow breath and waited a few more long moments, but he didn't become any more alert. When she realized that she'd been holding that breath in, she let it out in a sigh.

"It could be a while," came a voice from the doorway.

She glanced up at the nurse there. A thick-bodied woman in her forties, the nurse had a warm smile on an open, kindly face.

"Sometimes patients take a while to come out of it after so much blood loss," she explained. "But the doctor has him listed as stable. It looks like he's going to pull through just fine."

"Good," Carter whispered. Her throat was dry and her words stuck.

The nurse asked if she wanted any ice water.

Carter cleared her throat. "That'd be nice. Thank you."

The nurse smiled at her again. She looked at McNichol's chart, checked his tubes and tore off a printout from one of the machines. "Be right back."

Carter nodded her thanks.

Alone again, she looked down at McNichol. If she imagined him without the IV in his arm or the oxygen tubes in his nose, she could almost believe he was simply having a peaceful sleep. His face was still too white, though. And even though he was asleep, he looked haggard to her.

Have a look in the mirror, dearie, she thought sarcastically.

The nurse returned with a plastic cup filled with ice water. "There you go," she said.

"Thanks."

The nurse nodded, turned to go, then stopped. She gave Carter a long look. After a few moments, Carter raised her eyebrows questioningly. The nurse smiled. "Sorry," she said. "It's just…well, you're a cop, right?"

"I'm an FBI agent," Carter replied automatically, knowing that the distinction was lost on most people.

"Right," the nurse said. "I'm just…well, I just wanted to say that I admire what you do. I could *never* do your job."

Carter felt herself smiling. "I could never do *yours*," she said.

The nurse waved away her comment. "Oh, it's nothing. Check a few vitals, give out some medication." She pointed at Carter's cup. "Bring ice water. That's all. It's nothing like what you do. Like I said, I really admire what you do. It has to be hard."

"Thanks," Carter said. "But most days, it's no more difficult than what you just described."

"Not today," the nurse said quietly.

"No," Carter agreed. "Not today."

The nurse's eyes flicked to McNichol and back to Carter. "He's your partner?"

"Yes."

"And…not your husband or anything?"

Carter shook her head. "The Bureau would never allow that. Scott is married, though. His wife, Chelsea, is flying in from Florida."

"That's good," the nurse said. "Family usually brings a

good energy. Patients can sense it."

Carter nodded, not sure how to reply.

"You bring a good energy, too," the nurse said. "It's obvious that you care about him a lot."

Carter's eyes misted. "I do. He's a good friend."

The nurse smiled at her. "I'm sorry, hon. I didn't want to make you sad."

Carter wiped at her eyes. "It's okay."

The nurse took two steps toward her and rested her hand on Carter's shoulder. "My name's Brenda," she said.

"I'm Lori."

Brenda smiled. "You should feel good, Lori. You're the reason he's still alive."

Carter shrugged, but didn't answer.

"You are," Brenda insisted. "The doctor said so. So did the medics who brought him in. Everyone said that if you hadn't kept hard, direct pressure on that wound, he wouldn't have made it."

She squeezed Carter's shoulder.

"You saved his life."

Carter reached up and covered Brenda's hand with her own. "Thank you," she whispered.

Brenda gave her a final squeeze and turned to go.

"That's what he'll be saying when he wakes up," she said over her shoulder. "It just might be a little while before he gets around to it."

Carter smiled. Then she started laughing quietly. Brenda didn't notice and continued out of the room, closing the door quietly behind her.

Knowing Scott, Carter thought to herself, *it'll be six months before he mentions it.*

30

Sandy turned off the headlights as he turned onto Latawah. The space beneath the willow tree that he'd seen on the satellite photo was unoccupied, so he slid the Maverick to a stop directly beneath the limbs. The city kept the trees well-trimmed off of the roadways, but the slight overhang still gave him at least the illusion of some kind of cover.

He turned off the ignition and sat watching the small brick bungalow that belonged to Linda Valczinski. He listened to the ticking sound of the engine cooling and waited. This was a quiet, eclectic block of old Spokane. Unlike the Merchant neighborhood, which was fairly homogenous in the socio-economic status of it's inhabitants, Valczinski lived in the zone where middle class homes and rich dwellings co-existed side by side. People paid below market value for the big homes here but above market value for the small homes. This allowed for claims of simpler living for some and a bit of casual snobbery for others.

Would someone see the beater of a Ford Maverick he was driving and call it in as a suspicious vehicle? Or did everyone in this neighborhood mind their own business?

Sandy looked up and down the block, trying to gauge his exposure.

Then a light went on at Valczinski's house.

Sandy's gaze snapped to the small side porch where a single light blazed. A figure appeared at the door, clearly female. She locked the door, went down the steps and walked toward the garage.

Where was she going?

He paused, thinking. He could probably get to her before she left in her car. Force her back into the house. Hash out this whole sordid mess at gunpoint. Figure out why Larson – no, *Merchant* –went from being the Keeper to setting him up. Get to the bottom of this, and maybe even finish it.

He could do that.

Instead, he waited. A better plan was forming in his head. Follow her and see where that might lead. Was she going to meet Merchant? Sandy frowned. Maybe. She could be headed to the station, too, and that was the last place he'd want to follow her.

He decided to roll the dice and follow her.

The garage door rose and a dark blue Land Cruiser pulled out. She drove down the short driveway and turned right, heading north.

North was toward the police station.

Sandy waited until she was near the end of the block before starting the Maverick and following her. He pushed the small sinking feeling in his stomach aside. A lot of the city lay to the north. Just because she started that direction didn't mean she was headed for the police station.

He kept a reasonable distance, maintaining a visual on her Land Cruiser. They made their way to Grand Boulevard and headed north. Sandy followed. He calculated how far he'd follow her toward the police station before he peeled off. The problem he saw was that the closer he got to headquarters, the greater the volume of police traffic he'd encounter. He didn't believe the Maverick was on the radar yet, unless investigators had somehow traced him to the motel. Even then, would Arlo give up that he loaned his car? Sandy couldn't be sure, but he knew the sentiment on East Sprague was generally not to tell the police anything.

Valczinski stopped for the traffic light at Third Avenue, now on the southern fringe of downtown Spokane. Sandy eased the Maverick to a stop directly behind her. He averted his eyes, but watched her in his peripheral vision. She was checking out her reflection in the rearview mirror, primping her hair and touching up her lipstick. A thought struck him.

Why wasn't she driving her issued police car?

Unless times had changed radically, every lieutenant and above was issued an unmarked take-home police car. The vehicle was equipped with lights, siren and a police radio. He was sure Valczinski had driven something like that up to the homicide scene at the Merchant address. That's why the higher ranking members of the department had personally issued cars.

So why was she driving her personal vehicle instead of her G-ride?

The light turned green and Valczinski headed north, still toward the police station.

Sandy followed.

At Second Avenue, she turned left. Sandy bit his lip and renewed his consideration. Would he follow her across the Monroe Street bridge? The police station lay just a few blocks north of the river. If he crossed the bridge, he'd be right smack in the middle of all the comings and goings of the patrol vehicles.

Maybe he should—

Valczinski turned right on Post.

Sandy frowned. This was an odd route to take to headquarters.

A couple of blocks later, she pulled into a parking spot next to the Rutherford Hotel.

Sandy's frown disappeared.

She was meeting Merchant. She had to be.

If you're right about that, he reminded himself.

Sandy parked up the street. He watched her exit the Land Cruiser and jaywalk across the street to the hotel entrance. Once she disappeared from sight, he got out of the Maverick and walked directly toward the entrance himself.

The Rutherford Hotel was the grandest hotel in Spokane. Steeped in history dating back to the late 1800s, its ornate architecture and opulent surroundings always seemed out of reach to Sandy. This was a place where rich people met, where they conducted business and drank expensive liquor. It was where celebrities stayed when they travelled to Spokane and where the daughters of high society held wedding receptions.

It's just another hotel, Sandy told himself as he approached the oversized glass entrance doors. A man in a formal suit and top hat swung the door open for him.

"Good evening, sir," he said in a polished tone.

Sandy nodded back at him, hoping the doorman didn't watch the news. Or that his face would disappear into the sea of other faces the man encountered every shift.

He spotted Valczinski at the front desk. He drifted nearer, pretending to admire the carving work on the support beam along the wall. He kept his chin tucked low to his chest, just in case someone was watching on the security cameras. At the same time, he focused his hearing on the conversation between the desk clerk and Valczinski. He wasn't able to make out all of the words between them, but he caught a number.

Four-eleven.

Valczinski thanked him and moved to the white courtesy phone. Sandy didn't wait. He headed for the stairs.

Once he reached the fourth floor, he scouted the location of room 411. He found it near the end of the hall, just a few strides from the stairwell.

Perfect.

He propped the stairwell door open with his door and peered through the crack. He rested his hand on the .45 in his belt and waited.

A few minutes later, the ding of an elevator echoed down the hallway. Through the cracked door, he saw Valczinski approach. Her expression was one of self-satisfaction and anticipation. He waited until she used her key card to open the room door and push it open before he made his move.

In a smooth motion, he slipped through the stairwell door and power-walked toward Valczinski. She may have sensed him at the last moment because he saw her tense and turn slightly. He didn't hesitate. He used his hand to keep the door open and planted his foot in the small of her back. His thrusting kick sent her flying into the suite, tumbling forward off to the ground.

Sandy stepped inside, letting the door swing shut behind him. The quality hinges slowed the process and the door didn't slam, but closed with a solid click.

Valczinski lay motionless. Sandy stepped forward. At that moment, she whipped around, a small revolver clutched in both hands.

Sandy dropped to both knees and fired. The barrel flashed. The suppressor made a slapping thud noise. The metal slide clacked loudly.

Valczinski let out a cross between a grunt and muted cry and fell to her back. The revolver fell from her hands, making a subdued thump as it landed on the carpeted floor. She clutched at her knee, rocking on her back and moaning.

Sandy rose, took two steps and kicked the revolver. It skittered and hopped across the carpet like a football landing on its end, finally landing several feet away. Sandy was satisfied that the gun was outside her immediate reach and let it alone. A small kitchenette lined the wall to his left. He stepped around the mini-island , found a dish towel that was hanging from the stove handle and tossed it to her.

"It hurts like hell," he said, "but you're not going to die. Sit up and put pressure on it with that towel."

He didn't know what to expect of her, but she surprised him by sitting up and reaching for the towel. She folded it over clumsily with one hand and press down on her wounded knee. She gritted her teeth and breathed heavily, but made no further sounds of pain.

A warrior, Sandy thought. *Interesting*.

"I guess here is as good a place as any to talk," he said aloud. He walked around the kitchen island and squatted down like a baseball catcher, letting the .45 dangle from his hand.

Sandy could see her mind already at work, trying to determine his identity and his intent.

"I'm Sandy Banks," he told her. "Just to clear up any concerns you might have."

She blanched slightly, but recovered. "I've got nothing to say to you," Valczinski said through clenched teeth.

Sandy nodded. "Okay." He looked at her carefully, noting the lines in her face. He guessed she was approaching fifty. He tried to place her in the context of his time on the job, but couldn't.

"I don't remember you," he said. "When I left the job, twelve years ago, where were you?"

Valczinski didn't answer.

Sandy sighed. "You're a captain, so I'm going to assume you're an intelligent person. I know most working cops would disagree with that, but I figure you've got to take some tests to get as high up as you are, so you must be smart."

She flicked her eyes up at him, then back down at her wounded knee.

"Even if you're not that bright," Sandy went on, "you can't

be a cop and not have figured out something as simple as human motivation, right? So I'm going to make it simple enough for you." He pointed at his chest. "Right now, in poker terms, I'm what you would call 'all-in.' You know what that means?"

He was glad to see Valczinski give him a short nod.

"Good," he said. "In this case, it means I pretty much have nothing left to lose. You know what happened up at Merchant's house. You were up there."

Her eyes registered a moment of surprise, then realization. *She knows I watched the news,* Sandy thought. *Even in all that pain, she's a thinker.*

"So you know what I'm up against," Sandy continued. "For all I know, that FBI agent is dead and I'm facing a federal firing squad."

Valczinski shook her head. "He's alive."

"How do you know?"

"I called the field office," she said. "He's critical but stable."

Good, Sandy thought. Aloud, he said, "It doesn't matter. I'm in deep shit either way. My point is pretty simple. I want some answers. You're going to give them to me. If you don't…well, I don't have anything to lose here, do I? Like I said, I'm all in."

She stared at him warily.

He motioned to her knee. "And if it comes to that, the little boo-boo there will seem like a pleasant diversion, I can promise you."

After a few moments, she looked away and nodded her head. "Yes. Fine."

"Good." Sandy took a deep breath and let it out. "Let's start with where you were twelve years ago. Because like I said, I don't remember you."

"I was a sergeant in D.A.R.E.," she said.

Sandy nodded, considering. He wouldn't have paid much

attention to a unit like that. He'd been a graveyard officer, more concerned with taking doors and arresting bad guys.

"My name was Murray back then," she added.

"Maiden name?"

She shook her head. "Husband's name. Valczinski is my family name."

"So you're divorced."

"Over ten years now."

"What did you do before D.A.R.E.?"

Valczinski grimaced in pain and adjusted the pressure on her knee. "I worked undercover."

"Narco?"

She nodded. "Yeah, some of the time. And before I worked dope, I was in Vice."

Sandy gave her an appraising look. He imagined her fifteen years ago, dressed as a prostitute out on East Sprague. She'd probably been an effective lure. "That can be touch and go work," he observed.

"Sometimes."

"Get into any tight corners?"

"What cop hasn't?" she replied.

Sandy nodded. "True." *But undercover work is a special kind of danger,* he thought. "Looks like you fast-tracked to Captain," he said.

She shrugged. "Are you writing my biography or something?"

Sandy smiled at that. "No. I just want to know what I'm dealing with."

She didn't reply.

Sandy sat quietly for a moment, thinking. Then he asked, "What are you doing here?"

"Getting away from the grind."

"With who?"

"With myself," she said. "It's been a long day."

Sandy gave her a skeptical look. "Not meeting Lee?"

Her expression gave nothing away, but the flicker in her eyes told him everything.

"Lee who?" she asked, her tone almost convincing.

"Save it," Sandy said, playing out his partial bluff. "I know."

She hesitated, then said, "I'm not sure what you think you know, but –"

"I know that you're having an affair with Lee Merchant," Sandy interrupted. "I know he's one of your detectives. And I know that he manipulated me into killing his wife, Kelly."

Valczinski maintained her façade. "I don't know what you're talking about," she said. "But if you killed Kelly Merchant—"

"I killed her because the Keeper gave me a file," Sandy said in a quiet, forceful tone. "A fake file."

Valczinski's jaw set. "I don't know –"

Sandy leveled the gun at her. She stopped short.

"See," Sandy said, "this bullshit game isn't working for me. Way too much has happened. I'm in no fucking mood."

Valczinski swallowed. She looked down at the bloody dish towel that she held against her knee. "I should have never told him," she whispered. "Cal told me to never say a word to a single soul."

Sandy's eyes narrowed.

Cal?

"I should have just let the whole project die," she said.

"*You* should have…" he stared at her.

Valczinski stared back, her expression a mixture of anger and pain.

Sandy shook his head to clear his mind. "*You're* the Keeper?" he asked, bewildered.

Valczinski cleared her throat and looked up at him. She

saw the confusion in his face, then lowered her own eyes in defeat. "Jesus. You didn't know."

Sandy sat in stunned silence. He started to put the pieces together.

Valczinski raised her eyes again to meet his questioning stare. She shook her head. "Cal was smarter than you thought, wasn't he? Passing the baton to a woman like he did."

Sandy nodded slowly. It made sense to him now, though. Cal had been in almost every position there was on the department during his thirty-nine year career. And Sandy knew he'd spent a lot of time supervising the undercover units like Narcotics and Vice. Which was where he would have met Valczinski.

A thought occurred to him. "You and Cal weren't –"

Valczinski sniffed in disgust. "Are you kidding me? Cal was my rabbi, that's all. He looked out for me, brought me along. When he came down with the cancer, he took me aside and told me everything about the Four Horsemen. He turned it over to me. I was a brand new Lieutenant, working patrol at the time."

Sandy shook his head slowly. "We never knew who took over for Cal."

"I never knew who any of you were, either," she said. "Cal said it would be better that way for all of us."

"He was probably right," Sandy said. "But how did you find out about us?"

Valczinski sighed. "I only know about you and Brian Moore. I don't know who the other two are."

Are? Maybe she really doesn't know.

"How?" Sandy repeated.

"Simple," she said. "Lee tailed Brian from the drop box about a year ago. He tailed you on the Troy Collins job. After that, it was all just research. And I'm good at that."

Sandy watched her for a few quiet moments. "How's the

knee?" he asked.

"Hurts like hell," she answered.

He nodded. "Good."

"You're a bastard," she growled at him.

Sandy shook his head. "You have no idea. I killed Kelly Merchant, right? But what about Gail Ridley? Who killed her? You or Lee?"

He thought he saw some surprise come into her eyes, but he couldn't get a sure read on her. "Gail's dead?" she asked, her voice faltering.

"Shot in the head in her living room," Sandy said.

Valczinski turned a shade whiter and looked away. When she looked back, tears had formed in her eyes. "I didn't know," she said, her voice wavering. "It must have been Lee."

"I figured," Sandy said, watching her carefully.

She raised a bloody hand to her cheek and wiped away tears. The motion left a red smear across her cheekbone. "Gail was always good to me. And Cal loved her so much."

Sandy said nothing.

Valczinski wiped her eyes again, then slowly regained her composure. She swallowed and gave Sandy a steady gaze. "What else do you want to know?" she asked. "Do you want to know why?"

"Why Lee killed Gail? I think I know."

"No," she said. "Why I gave you the false file for Kelly Merchant."

"I think I know that, too."

Valczinski nodded. "It was for love, you know."

Sandy gave her a puzzled look. "*Love?* How can you say that?"

Her expression became defensive. "Because it's true. Lee and I love each other. The only way we could be together is if his wife was gone."

"You never heard of divorce?"

She shook her head. "I wanted him to divorce her, but that wasn't an option. He'd lose a fortune. The house was in her name. So were most of their investments. Plus, he said his kids would hate him forever if he divorced their mother."

"So you *kill* her?" Sandy shook his head in amazement. "When exactly did that seem like a sane decision?"

She mirrored his amazement with her own. "Seriously? You're going to sit there and pass judgment? After all the people you've killed over the past how many years?"

"Those were evil men," Sandy said. "They earned their fate."

Valczinski actually laughed, letting out a short, barking sound. "You stole that line from Cal," she said. "Those were his exact words when he was justifying this whole sick project to me ten years ago. And I bought it." Her laughter died off. "No, you don't get to judge. You didn't know Lee's wife. Little Miss Perfect for the world to see, but she put him through hell."

"She didn't deserve to die."

"How do you know?" Valczinski snapped at him.

Sandy shrugged. "It doesn't matter," he said. He rose from his crouch and reached for the telephone on the nightstand next to the bed. Valczinski watched him with wary eyes.

"The game is over," he said as he dialed.

31

A buzzing sound woke Carter from a light doze. She still sat in the chair next to McNichol's bed. She glanced at her watch. Nine-twenty. Still almost an hour before she had to call Maw and check in.

If she even decided to.

The buzzing sound came again. She followed the sound to the small plastic bin at the head of the bed containing all of McNichol's personal belongings. She realized after a moment that it was his cell phone.

It could be Chelsea, she thought. Maybe she was able to get on an earlier flight.

She reached into the bin and picked up the phone. The caller ID read "Rutherford Hotel."

Carter frowned. There's no way Chelsea would have checked into a hotel before calling. So who was calling Scott from the Rutherford?

She opened the phone. "Hello?" she said cautiously.

The line was quiet for a moment. Then a male voice asked, "I'm calling for the FBI. Who's this?"

"Agent Lori Carter," she automatically responded, forcing her tone professional. "Who are you?"

"Agent Carter, this is Sandy Banks."

Carter remained silent, surprise taking her voice.

"I heard that Agent McNichol is in stable condition," the

voice said. "I'm glad to hear that."

Carter's mind flew into action. She reached for her own cell phone. She had to order a trace as quickly as possible, just in case the caller ID was spoofed. Meanwhile she had to keep Banks on the line. "Thanks," she said, though the words stuck in her throat and barely came out.

"I know you don't mean that," Banks said. "I wouldn't, either, in your position."

Carter flipped open her phone and accessed her contact list. "No, I do mean it," she said.

"No, you don't," Banks said. "Let's keep this call honest, okay? I'm only going to be on for another ten seconds, so don't bother with a trace."

Carter didn't pause but continued to scroll down her list to the all-hours number for the computer geeks.

"I'll tell you where I am, anyway, and save you the trouble."

I know where you are, she thought. Aloud, she said, "I'm listening," and pulled a pen from her pocket.

"I'm at the Rutherford Hotel in room number four-eleven. I'm with Captain Linda Valczinski. She's city police."

Carter held the phone in the crook of her shoulder and scrawled 4-1-1 furiously on the palm of her hand.

"And since you know pretty much everything else, I'll tell you this, too. She's the Keeper."

Carter stopped, surprised.

"She and Lee Merchant set me up to kill his wife," Banks told her. "And one of them killed Gail Ridley."

Gail who?

"Probably Merchant, if you want my take on it," Banks said.

"Wait a minute," Carter started to say, but Banks interrupted.

"I don't have a minute," he said. "I don't have any time left at all."

The line went dead.

Carter stared down at the phone in her hand. She processed the information quickly, then considered her options.

If Banks was telling the truth—

Why would he lie now?

—and a city police captain and detective were dirty on this, she needed to use State Patrol for uniform presence. And who could she trust on the Bureau?

Not Maw. She'd call him from the house, after she'd detained Valczinski. If Banks was lying—

He's not. I know it.

—then it would mean her career. From what Maw said earlier, her career was fairly well in the toilet anyway. But if she busted this case wide open, he would have no choice but to give her her due. It might piss him off something fierce, but in the end, he would bow to the results. And taking down a vigilante operation like the Four Horsemen was the kind of thing that made careers for people like Maw.

And saved them for people like me, Carter thought.

She reached out and squeezed McNichol's hand. "Hang in there, Scott," she whispered. "I'll see you after."

32

Sandy hung up the phone. Valczinski stared at him, a mixture of surprise and anger on her face.

"Why would you do that?" she asked.

Sandy let a small smile touch his lips. "For justice," he said quietly.

"Don't give me that shit," Valczinski said, her eyes narrowing. "There's no such thing."

Sandy shrugged. "Maybe not. But you're still going to face something like it."

"Don't be so sure," she muttered.

Before Sandy could reply, he heard a beep behind him and the clicking sound of the door lock disengaging.

"Don't move," he hissed at Valczinski. He moved quickly into the kitchenette, taking up the best angle he could find. A moment later, Lee Merchant stepped through the door.

His face bore the same self-satisfied grin Sandy had seen on Valczinski's face as she came down the hall a short time ago. Merchant glanced down at her on the ground with the bloody towel pressed to her knee. His expression turned to grim surprise. His hand snaked under his left armpit.

"Don't move!" Sandy barked at him.

Merchant froze.

"Move your hand away from the gun," Sandy ordered.

Merchant slowly withdrew his empty hand from under his

light jacket.

Sandy heard shuffling sounds on the floor. He glanced over at Valczinski. She was scrambling toward the revolver further into the living room. He swung his aim onto her. Then he saw a flash of movement to his right.

Merchant was going for his gun again.

Sandy swung the muzzle back toward Merchant. "Don't!" he yelled.

Merchant froze.

Sandy stepped forward and dropped into a crouch again. He had a clear view of Merchant from this position, but the counter hid him from Valczinski. Merchant's eyes gave away her position. His smile gave away that she'd reached the pistol.

"Don't come any closer," Sandy told her. "I will put two slugs into his chest if I hear you moving this way."

He strained with his ears, but all he could hear was the slight hum of the mini-fridge and her labored breathing.

Merchant turned his eyes toward Sandy. "Well, I guess we have ourselves a bit of a Mexican standoff here."

Sandy looked into Merchant's self-assured eyes. Disgust and rage bubbled up from the pit of his stomach.

"You need to move, Lee," Valczinski said. "Just come to me."

Merchant shook his head. "No, he'll shoot. I believe he actually will shoot."

"Please, Lee," she begged. Her voice sounded thick with tears. "Come this way."

Merchant smiled slightly, ignoring her. "What do we do now, Banks? This is your game. How do you want to play it?"

"I've already played it," Banks said. He moved his index finger onto the trigger. The pressure required to depress the trigger was minimal. A few small pounds, was all. Just squeeze gently and he could send Lee Merchant to hell.

He clenched his jaw. Started to squeeze.

He stopped and let up.

Merchant smiled more widely at him. "Lost your taste for it, huh?"

"Go for your gun," Sandy said in a low voice, "and you'll find out."

Merchant looked back at Valczinski. "He's lost his nerve, baby."

Sandy put his finger back on the trigger. He thought of Gail Ridley's blank stare at the ceiling. Her slack jaw.

I should kill this son of a bitch.

Merchant looked back. Some of the confidence went out of his eyes, but he maintained his façade. "You've got a curious set of morals, Banks," he said. "I'll give you that."

"It's over," Sandy told him.

"Oh, I know," Merchant said, smiling broadly again. "Thanks to you, it is. Now you can go your merry way and leave Linda and I to go ours. But I'd get out of town if I were you. The feds are going to be on your ass for a while."

"The feds are on their way here right now," Sandy told him.

"Bullshit," he scoffed.

"I just called them thirty seconds ago. Ask her."

Merchant eyed the telephone on the counter, then turned his gaze toward Valczinski.

"He did," she said. "At least, he called someone right before you came in."

Sandy pinpointed her location from her voice. She hadn't moved more than a foot or two from where he'd kicked the revolver to.

Merchant looked back down at Sandy. "What the hell are you trying to pull?"

"Like I said, it's over."

"Why bring the feds into it? We could still all get out of

this clean."

"The feds are already into it," Sandy said. "They've got Brian. He flipped. He's their confidential informant."

Merchant looked stunned.

"They're up on the whole thing," Sandy told him. "The FBI is going to blow the Four Horsemen project wide open."

Merchant shook his head slightly. After a few moments, he stammered, "Are you sure—"

"I'm just as fucked as you are right now," Sandy said.

Merchant looked back and forth between Sandy and Valczinski. "No," he said, "there's something more here. There has to be." He pointed at Banks. "You're CIA or some shit, aren't you?"

Sandy frowned. "CIA? Please."

"No, it has to be," Merchant said. "This is all too convenient."

"It doesn't seem very convenient to me," Sandy said, "considering we're all going to prison."

"No way. You're in on it, aren't you?"

"I'm in it up to my neck," Sandy answered. "Unfortunately, it's the same shit creek you're in."

"I know about your bogus military file," Merchant blurted out. "Something more is going on here."

Sandy's jaw set. How had Merchant gotten access to military files?

It didn't matter, he decided. It was all a dead end, anyway.

"What military file?" Valczinski asked Merchant.

"My name is Sandy Banks," he said. "That's who I am."

"Bullshit," Merchant said. A droplet of sweat appeared at his temple and rolled down the side of his face. "You're undercover or something. This is a set up."

"Undercover?" Sandy almost laughed. How many ways was *that* true? But not in the way Merchant obviously thought. "No," he said. "But we are running out of time here."

Merchant wiped away the sweat with his sleeve. He looked frantically back and forth between Sandy and Valczinski, as if he were weighing a decision. Then he pointed at her. "You know she's the Keeper, right?"

"Lee!" Valczinski said his name in a tone full of surprise and hurt.

Merchant ignored her. "I'm just a lackey, Banks. Or whatever your name is. I didn't know who was in that last file. She hired me to meet with you and make sure you followed through, but I had no idea what she was planning."

Sandy said nothing. He kept his gun trained on Merchant. Another pair of sweat droplets rose on his opposite temple. Sandy could hear a soft sob from the living room.

"You have to believe me," Merchant said.

In the distance, the tell-tale sound of police sirens began to sing.

Merchant held out his hands toward Sandy plaintively. "Please," he said. "I had no idea."

"You're a liar," Sandy said.

"No." Merchant shook his head forcefully. "I'm telling the truth."

"What about Gail Ridley?"

"Who?"

"Don't lie to me!" Sandy snarled. "I know you were at her house. She told me."

Merchant held up his hands apologetically. "Okay, yeah. I went to see her. I thought she might have some information about you guys, since she was Cal's old lady. But she didn't know anything."

"She knew enough. She knew who you were. And you murdered her."

"No. It wasn't me. I swear to God."

"I don't believe you."

"I wasn't the one who shot her, man." Tears rose up in

Merchant's eyes. "Please, Banks, or whoever you are. You have to believe me. I didn't kill anyone."

Sandy glared at him. "I never said she was shot. How'd you know that was how she was murdered?"

Merchant's eye twitched. "I-I didn't know anything," he stammered. "I just—"

"Shut up," Sandy said. "I don't want to hear any more of your lies. Just wait for the police to get here."

Merchant's face grew even more panicked. "Listen, I'll turn State's Witness. I'll testify." He searched out Sandy's face, his eyes imploring. "I will."

Sandy looked at him, disbelieving. "You never quit, do you?"

Merchant ignored his statement. "I know everything. Dates, places, names, everything." He ticked items off on his fingers as he spoke. "I'll give it all up. I'll go to court and—"

A shot rang out.

Sandy jumped, but immediately saw where it had struck.

Another shot blast filled the small suite. Merchant staggered back into the wall next to the door. He sank to the ground, sliding against the wall. His face bore a baffled expression, tinged with disbelief. His mouth hung open and he seemed to be trying to finish his final sentence. Instead, only a light wheeze came out. His open eyes became a fixed stare.

There was a moment's pause, then three more shots rang out. These came whizzing through the wooden cabinet between him and Valczinski. He heard one ricochet off of a pan inside the cupboard. Another one skipped past his foot, missing him by an inch.

The sound of the shots faded, followed by several metallic clicks. Sandy rose and swung around the cabinet, leveling his .45 at Valczinski. She held the small revolver out at an arm's length, squeezing the trigger repeatedly. When she saw Sandy's gun pointed at her, she let her hand fall to her side.

The pistol clunked mutely on the carpet.

"Finish it," she told him, her voice full of surrender.

Sandy looked at her long and hard. Then he glanced at Merchant's still frame pitched awkwardly against the wall. The sirens were growing closer. He looked at Valczinski again.

"It *is* finished," he said.

He turned away from her. He walked past Merchant's still body next to the door. He slipped his .45 under his shirt as he opened the door and stepped into the hallway. At the head of the stairs, he pulled the fire alarm. The shrill clanging sound filled the hotel. He entered the stairwell and started downward. By the time he reached the main floor, confused and frightened guests littered the lobby. He melted easily into the crowd.

At the front doors, he flowed outside with the other panicked patrons, never looking back.

33

Special Agent Lori Carter sipped the coffee one of the State detectives had handed her. It was rich and textured, unlike the slightly burned taste of cheap convenience store brew that she was used to on crime scenes and stakeouts. One of the perks of investigating a homicide at a five star hotel, she figured.

Carter flipped open her phone and dialed the hospital. Someone with a friendly voice answered on the second ring. "ICU, Nurse's Station."

"Is this Brenda?" Carter asked.

"It is."

"Brenda, it's Lori Carter," she said. "I'm just calling to check on my partner, Agent McNichol."

"Oh, hi there, Lori. He's fine. I just checked on him less than five minutes ago. In fact, his wife has arrived and is with him right now."

"Good. Thanks."

"You're welcome."

Carter smiled at Brenda's warm tone. She hung up and slipped her phone in her pocket.

The statie exited room 411 and walked down the hall towards her, ducking under the crime scene tape. "The male is DOA, no question. Looks like two small caliber shots to the sternum."

"Shot through the heart," Carter mused.

"Pretty much."

"And Valczinski?"

He rubbed the short hair on top of his head. "I've got two troopers with her up at the hospital. Her knee looked nasty but nothing fatal."

"The troopers will stay with her?"

He smiled. "Oh, yes, ma'am. They'll gown up and go into the operating room, if necessary."

"Doctors won't like that," Carter said.

The statie shrugged. "My troopers won't care. Give a trooper a mission, he carries it out."

Carter nodded, satisfied. "Did she say anything?"

"Nothing very coherent. I think she was going into shock from the gunshot wound."

"What did she say?"

"Something about being Lee's keeper, I think. Lee's the DOA. Detective Lee Merchant."

Carter sipped her coffee, trying to disguise her anticipation. "What was it she said about being the keeper again?"

"I don't know for sure. The first trooper on scene wrote it down exactly." He fished out a piece of notepaper from his breast pocket and looked at it a moment. Then he read, "Oh, Lee. I'm sorry I was ever the keeper. Sorry for everything." He glanced up at her. "Mean anything to you?"

Carter nodded and took the slip of paper from him. "Means everything," she said.

The statie looked at her, waiting for an explanation. When she didn't provide one, he shrugged. "Okay, well, I've got a crime scene to work. My forensics people are about five minutes out. My CO called the Chief of Police, so I'd expect some city people to start showing up here pretty soon." He shook his head. "I don't know how happy they're going to be, seeing as how it's one of their own dead inside and another one up at the hospital."

"You don't want their help, I take it?"

He shook his head. "I don't need it. And with their people involved, it's probably cleaner if no police personnel even come onto this floor, much less into the crime scene."

"Well, if you have enough troopers to protect the scene," Carter said. "I think I have the right person to deal with the locals."

"I'm a little short on troopers, but I've called the Sheriff for a few deputies to maintain the outer perimeter. We'll handle the scene itself and the prisoner."

"And I'll provide federal oversight," Carter said. "Just so no one can make any claims of collusion. Besides, this is officially a corruption case now."

"You got it," the statie said. He turned and headed back down the hall toward the crime scene.

Carter withdrew her phone and dialed again. Someone answered on the second ring for this call, but there was no warmth in the voice.

"Special Agent-in-Charge Maw," he snapped.

"This is Carter."

"I can see that on my Caller ID. What the hell is going on? I just got a call from the commanding officer of the State Patrol Barracks telling me that he has deployed an investigative team in support of our operation inside the city."

"That's correct."

"He said that it was at the Rutherford Hotel."

"Also correct."

"I'm on my way to the scene," Maw told her.

"That's good."

"You want to tell me what the hell you think you're doing, Agent Carter? Besides pissing away your career?"

Carter smiled to herself. "Actually, sir, I think my career is doing just fine. And unfortunately, yours is about to get a huge boost, as well."

"What do you mean? Explain yourself."

"I've got the Keeper," Carter said. "And I've solved the Kelly Merchant murder."

"What?"

"You heard me."

There was a short silence, then Maw cleared his throat. "Well, what about Banks?"

"He's in the wind for now."

"Well, that's…that's just unacceptable."

"Listen," Carter snapped. "I've just busted this case wide open, dickhead. And if you want to come take credit for it, you better get your scrawny ass over here and be nice to me. Or my official report won't say a thing about your critical involvement and stellar leadership in making this happen."

The other end of the line was silent for a long moment. Carter considered hanging up on the arrogant bastard, but she hung on out of curiosity.

Maw cleared his throat again.

"I'm, uh, about fifteen minutes away."

"Super," Carter said, smiling.

"Is the media on scene yet?"

"They will be by the time you get here."

"I'll, uh, I'll take care of that angle then."

"Super again," Carter said, her smile spreading. "And I'll need you to keep the local police at bay so the State Patrol can conduct their investigation. With Bureau oversight, of course."

"Of course. I'll take care of it." There was another pause. Then Maw said in a forced tone, "And, uh, good job, Agent Carter."

"Thank you, asshole," Carter said.

And this time, she did hang up.

34

Sandy glanced out of the Greyhound bus window. The two lane highway was lined with trees. The view was beautiful, even to his red scratchy eyes, but more than that, the nature of the route felt safe. It felt far away from Spokane, the Horsemen, all of it.

He'd driven poor Arlo's Maverick out of town, where he'd picked up his false ID and extra cash. Then he drove as far as Ritzville before hopping on the first bus. He'd headed south and now east via what he and his army buddies always called 'the big gray dog.'

Get a window seat was the advice every soldier gave the other.

The state highway eastbound through southern Idaho wasn't the fastest route home, but it was the smartest. He knew the FBI wouldn't stop looking for him, but he guessed that they'd be more concerned with unraveling the mess of the Four Horsemen project than initiating a manhunt for him. Especially since McNichol had survived and he'd served up Merchant and Valczinski to them on a silver platter.

He wasn't home free. He still had to be careful. A haircut and a change of clothes in Ritzville helped. Keep a low profile. Find his way home. That was probably the safest place in the world right now, since no one knew where that was. Not

Brian. Not the FBI. Not even the Army, unless he'd been betrayed there as well.

No chance, he thought. *Some vows are too sacred.*

Still, Merchant got his information from someone. Who?

Probably some clerk at Central Files, Sandy figured. Someone smart enough to guess that the file was bogus, but not someone who knew why.

No, home was safe. He was sure of it.

He wondered if Janet received his letter. He tried to imagine her reaction, but after so many years, there were just too many possibilities. Wondering about things like that was a waste of time. He'd know in a few days. A week at most.

Instead, he let the distance between him and Spokane mount, one diesel fueled, gray dog mile at a time. He left the Horsemen behind. He left Brian behind. He let it all go with every tree that flitted by the window.

He felt free.

Almost…*free.*

Twinges of guilt worked at the edges of his conscience. He pushed them away as best he could. For the first time since Cal died, he actually felt the beginnings of new hope. Maybe there was a life for him left in this world.

Just maybe.

The trees gave way on his side of the road. A huge silver swath of water opened up to the right. The early morning light danced across the wide river, sparkling. He remembered the last time he'd felt this kind of renewed hope. There'd been the same kind of light on the water then, too. Maybe it was some kind of a sign.

Sandy smiled.

Epilogue

Cal Ridley drove his truck northward in silence. The hum of the engine filled the cab. The long gear stick vibrated under his hand. The darkness of early morning had begun to fade as dawn crept in from the eastern sky.

Beside him sat Sandy Banks, also silent. Cal guessed him at about thirty-five or so, though the hard lines of his face either said that he had another five years than that or some hard mileage. Cal guessed it was the latter.

The two hadn't spoken since Cal gassed up at the small corner convenience store. He'd handed Sandy a cup of hot, black coffee in a Styrofoam cup. Sandy thanked him for it. That was the sum total of the words between them this morning.

Yesterday hadn't been much more verbose. Cal called Sandy on the phone around six o'clock, just after he and Gail had eaten dinner.

"You ever fish, son?" he asked, after identifying himself.

"Not that I recall, Lieutenant," Sandy replied. Cal could hear the liquor in his voice, even though it was carefully controlled. He shrugged. The man was under a lot of stress. The Internal Affairs case involving the death of a domestic violence victim after he'd been at the house on a patrol call for service was still pending. A few drinks might help take the edge off at a time like this. Besides, Gail was in the kitchen pouring coffee and mixing in Bailey's Irish Crème, so who was he to criticize another man's drinking habits?

"I'm going fishing up at Horseshoe Lake tomorrow morning," Cal told him. "I think you should come with me."

"Yeah?"

"Yeah."

There was a pause, then Sandy said, "I don't have any gear."

"I've got extra," Cal told him. "I'll be by your place at 5:30 sharp."

"You know where I live?"

"Of course," Cal replied. "See you in the morning." Then he'd hung up.

Now, riding quietly together in the cab of Cal's truck, he was surprised that the man beside him had yet to ask any questions. Most men didn't have that kind of patience. Particularly when the pressure was on.

Maybe he is right for the job, Cal thought.

At the lake, he found the public access area deserted. It was a long drive up a dirt road to get to the lake, so it wasn't popular to begin with. On a Wednesday morning, anyone out of bed this early was probably looking for a tee time and not a boat launch.

Cal backed the truck down to the water. He untied the harness. Without a word, Sandy helped him lift the little rowboat out of the bed and lower it into the water. Cal grabbed the tackle box and two poles and loaded them into the boat. He pointed at the red ice chest. Sandy grabbed it and put it in the center of the boat.

Sandy waited by the boat as Cal parked the truck. Cal walked down to the launch, his boots making loud crunching noises on the dirt and gravel as he approached. When he was getting close, Sandy finally asked him a question.

"What's this all about, sir?" His voice was level and matter of fact.

Cal gave him a tight grin and shook his head. "Some things are better discussed out on the lake."

"Why's that?"

"Fish don't have ears."

Sandy didn't laugh, but he didn't question Cal, either. The two men clambered into the boat. Cal pushed off. He clicked on the tiny outboard motor that ran off a car battery. No gas engines were allowed on this lake, which was one more reason why it was his favorite place to fish.

Cal headed straight out to the center of the lake. The two men rode in silence, almost a re-enactment of the trip to the lake in Cal's truck. When he finally cut the little motor, the boat continued to drift slowly in the direction of travel.

"I brought you a closed face reel," Cal told him, holding the pole out. "You know how to use that?"

Sandy shrugged, took the pole and examined the device. "Push the button to cast, release and reel in?"

"Exactly. Give me your hook."

Sandy unhooked the barb from the eyelet and held it out toward Cal. The veteran lieutenant threaded a worm onto it expertly. "Throw that out there and see what happens."

Sandy flicked the pole, sending the hook and bobber a fair distance from the boat.

"Nice," Cal grunted, then set his own hook. He cast off in the opposite direction.

They sat for a while in silence again. Sandy stared at his bobber. Cal twisted open a small flask and added some Bailey's Irish Crème to his lukewarm coffee. He sipped it a few times. Finally, he said, "You got yourself into a bit of a jackpot, didn't you?"

Sandy glanced over at him. "Yeah," was all he said.

Jesus, Cal thought. *This kid really holds things inside.*

Except he wasn't a kid, even if he seemed like it to Cal. He was a man, a cop. And according to his personnel file, a veteran of the war in the Middle East. Cal wondered if what Sandy had seen there had anything to do with how closed off he seemed now.

"You talk to the shrink about it yet?" he asked.

Sandy nodded.

"And?"

Sandy actually smiled slightly, though there was a certain darkness to the expression. "Isn't that supposed to be confidential, Lieutenant?"

"It is," Cal said. "But out here, I'm just Cal. And we're just fishing."

Sandy eyed him for a long moment, as if gauging his sincerity. Finally, he said, "I told the doctor what he needed to hear so that he could tell the Chief what he needed to hear."

"So that you could get back to work," Cal finished for him.

"Exactly. If that's where things are going."

"But you didn't tell him the truth."

Sandy took a deep breath and let it out. "What's the truth, anyway?"

"I think," Cal said, "that the truth is you did the best you could do."

Sandy shook his head. "No. I made a mistake. Because of that, an innocent woman died. If I'd done the best I could do, she'd still be alive. And the guy that killed her would be in jail. Not on the run in some other state."

"I read the reports," Cal said. "Sounds to me like you did what anyone else would have done. There was no reason to believe she was lying to you about him being in the house."

"I should have searched the place," Sandy said. "I had probable cause to arrest him for domestic violence assault. I should have been sure he wasn't there."

"I imagine she was pretty convincing."

"She was scared to death of him." Sandy shook his head.

"If nothing else, I should have waited until she left to her sister's house. I should have made sure she was safe."

"Maybe," Cal relented. "But it was an honest mistake. We all make mistakes."

Sandy met his eyes. His own were hard, but full of pain. "Don't you understand? I *failed* her. And the cost of that failure was her life."

"I have it on good authority that the review panel is going to clear you of any wrongdoing on this," Cal told him. "You'll get reprimanded for negligence, plus forty hours of suspension. But they won't find any malice. You won't lose your job."

"It doesn't matter what they say. I don't deserve to carry a badge," Sandy said. "I'm think I'm going to quit."

"Now you're feeling a little bit sorry for yourself," Cal told him. The end of his line twitched. "Oh, there you go. A little nibble."

He felt Sandy staring at him, but he focused on the end of his pole. When nothing happened after a while, he sighed. "Either too smart or not hungry enough," he said with no hint of dejection. The fish would be back. Or another one would.

He looked over at Sandy. "You have to move on, son. You can't carry the weight of these things around with you. Mistakes happen. Make up for it if you want, but don't carry it around like this."

Sandy stared at him, but his expression softened. He surprised Cal, as tears formed in his eyes but didn't fall. "Some mistakes are too big to let go," he said, his voice cracking.

Cal got the distinct impression he wasn't talking about the domestic violence victim from a week ago.

This kid has been through some kind of hell, he realized. Was it his father that did this to him? His mother? Or a woman he loved? Whoever it was, the DV victim last week was not the first time Sandy Banks had failed someone important to him with disastrous results. Cal was certain of it.

"Who did you fail?" he asked in a low voice. "Who was it?"

Sandy shook his head. A couple of tears fell heavily from his cheeks and splatted on the floor of the boat. He wiped his eyes. "It doesn't matter. I can never make it right. It's too late."

"Maybe," Cal said. "But maybe not."

"No," Sandy replied. "It's too late."

"It's never too late for redemption, son," Cal said. "My wife assures me of that every Sunday."

Another nibble came at the end of Cal's pole, followed by a large bend. He felt the familiar vibrations of a fish on the line, but he didn't reel it in right away. Instead, he ignored it, and watched Sandy.

Sandy returned his stare with an open and frank gaze.

Cal smiled. "Son, here is what is going to happen. I'm going to reel in this fine specimen of rainbow trout. And then I'm going to tell you about something special that you were tailor-made to be a part of. A way you might be able to make up for some of those mistakes you won't let go of."

"What are you talking about?"

"Justice," Cal said, turning the knob on his reel. "I'm talking about a little bit of justice."

ABOUT THE AUTHOR

Frank was a police officer from 1993 to 2013, retiring as a captain. After retirement, he taught leadership at police agencies across the US and Canada for four years, before retiring completely in order to write full time. He is the author of over two dozen crime novels.

In addition to writing, Frank is an avid hockey fan and a tortured guitarist. He lives in Redmond, Oregon, with his wife, who remains simultaneously his biggest fan and critic.

You can keep up with him at http://frankzafiro.com.